BEAST BENEATH THE SKIN

Born in North Middlesex Hospital on 25th September 1961, Thomas Bloor has lived for most of his life in various parts of the London Borough of Waltham Forest. He took a degree in Fine Art at North East London Polytechnic and has worked as a school librarian, an art technician, a classroom assistant and an artificial flower maker. He now does some part-time teaching and editorial work but devotes most of his time to writing. He currently lives in Walthamstow with his wife, two daughters and two cats.

Also by **Thomas Bloor**:

WORM in the BLOOD

BEAST
BENEATH
THE
SKIN

Novel and illustrations by

Thomas Bloor

ff

faber and faber

First published in 2006
by Faber and Faber Limited
3 Queen Square London WC1N 3AU

Typeset by Faber and Faber Limited
Printed in England by Mackays of Chatham plc, Chatham, Kent

A CIP record for this book
is available from the British Library

ISBN 978–0–571–23111–9
ISBN 0–571–23111–X

2 4 6 8 10 9 7 5 3 1

Thanks to Elaine, Joanna and Louise and also to
Kathryn and Claire

For Theo, Ellie and Joe

I

Scattered Ash

A BOOK BURNING

The book lay open among the ashes. The buckled pages, charred and flecked with soot, trembled now in the breeze that blew through the old warehouse. The mouths of grazing snails had reduced the page corners to mulch. Woodlice slept beneath the shade of the back cover.

An extra strong gust of wind ruffled through the pages and flipped the book closed. Just discernible on the fire-blackened cover was the word DIARY and underneath, written in large, looping handwriting, a name: Adda-Leigh MacDuff.

SMOKE OR CLOUD

The Oriental priest paced the floor, hands clasped behind his back. Sam listened for the clunk of the loose floorboard as the small man stepped back and forth across the room.

'There is much that you have to learn, Sam,' Father David said. 'We must draw up a new schedule of study and, this time, we must keep to it.'

Sam sighed, his breath hissing out across two rows of spitefully sharp teeth. A thin plume of white smoke dissipated in the stifling air of the room.

'Do you really have to do that?' Father David knitted his brows. There was a hint of exasperation in his voice.

'Yes.' Sam lay slouched across the old sofa. The rough, scaly skin on his arms caught on the upholstery.

'I've got an itchy throat,' he muttered.

'Then why the smoke? It'll only make it worse!' Father David turned and paced back to the table. 'You shouldn't breathe fire at all, if truth be told.'

'Why not?' Sam jerked his head around to look at the priest.

'It's not . . .' Father David paused uncertainly but then continued anyway. 'It's not traditional.'

'Welsh dragons breathe fire, don't they?' Sam's voice was deep, rasping and sullen. He narrowed his eyes. 'I'm only half Luhngdonese, remember? The rest of me is all Welsh!'

Father David sighed. 'The western notion of the fire-breathing dragon is based on a misinterpretation of the clouds depicted around the mouths of Chinese dragons. Dragons make clouds, not fire. They bring rain, not destruction. They are a force for good, and not for evil.'

Sam let out a contemptuous snort. A hot, sulphurous smell filled the room.

'I am going to write out a new schedule. A seven-day timetable,' Father David said, pacing the floor again. 'You must learn to stand alone, Sam. I may not always be here. Mrs Hare, remember, was killed because she helped me find you. We were lucky to get to Ireland undetected. Who knows how long we'll be safe?'

'Whatever.' Sam's voice was a low, surly rumble. He coughed, hawked, and expelled a ragged smoke ring through one nostril. Leaning over, he spat a globule of damply smouldering ash into the wastepaper bin.

He turned his face to the wall.

Father David sighed again.

'Sam, go and fetch a bucket of water and a damp cloth.' His voice was even, if a little weary. 'You've just set fire to the wastepaper bin again.'

CLOSING DOWN
AND MOVING OUT

The horse cropped the grass, tugging up mouthfuls, tearing at the overgrown lawn. The last house on Tow Road was empty. The back fence was broken down and the end of the garden was filled with a great heap of rubble, topped by an old electric fire and a mildewed mattress.

Georgette had dismounted and led Dandelion around the piled-up refuse to let the horse graze on the overgrown lawn. She supposed someone had once cared for the garden, cut the grass with a mower, planted roses in the borders, put down slug pellets to protect the flowers and breadcrumbs to feed the birds. Not any more. The garden was a wasteland, and the house was a dark, looming shape, as lifeless and threatening as a windswept crag on some desolate moor.

Everything had changed. A few doors away the Ferryman's Arms was in darkness. The pub sold its last pint a month ago and was now closed for good. Scaffolding covered the frontage. The owners would have demolished it and sold the site as real estate, but the glazed tiling in the Gents toilets was of sufficient interest to scholars of Victorian architecture to have a preservation order put on it. Georgette's father had been kept on as a temporary caretaker while the owners decided what to do with the building. He spent his days looking for a more permanent job, morosely filling in application forms and ploughing through newspaper advertisements. He'd yet to be granted so much as an interview. The one thing worse than living in a pub, Georgette thought, was living in a closed-down pub.

The stables under the flyover, too, were facing closure. The rent asked for the dank space between the concrete piles beneath the motorway had become too dear. It seemed there weren't enough people keen to pay money to ride a horse around a piece of urban waste ground. Dandelion, the horse Georgette had ridden for the past two years, was to be moved to a livery stable somewhere in Essex. This nocturnal ride through the dark streets that bordered the canal and the marshes was to be the last time Georgette rode on Dandelion.

The impending loss of her horse and her home were bitter blows to Georgette and they would have consumed her every thought had it not been for another loss, one that cast a shadow over the whole of Marshside. Georgette's closest friend had gone missing two weeks before. Adda-Leigh had disappeared.

Georgette stood in the darkness of the overgrown garden. The scent of the grass and the warm, rich aroma of horse filled her nostrils but failed to comfort her. Dandelion would soon be gone and Adda-Leigh was nowhere to be found.

'Where are you, Addy?' Georgette whispered into Dandelion's mane. 'What's happened to you?'

The horse continued to crop the grass, unconcerned. Georgette turned away and stared bleakly up at the dark and empty building that had once been a home, but that now stood as silent as a tomb.

ILL WIND

She was in darkness. Total darkness. She felt the air gathering, moving and shifting, filling the cell she sat in, seeming to animate the dark around her. But there was no freshness to this wind. It seemed to emanate from somewhere deep beneath the earth. Warm and fetid, the wind filled the cell with airborne grit. Adda-Leigh closed her eyes against the sting of dust and the dryness of the pressing air. This, she thought, is how it must feel to be on the inside of an enormous party balloon, blown up by a particularly foul-breathed giant.

Then came the sound. It began as a faint hiss, was joined by a vibrating hum, then an echoing rattle, building to a mechanical moan that finally died to a string of broken whispers, then silence again. Adda-

Leigh knew the sound well enough. An Underground train had gone by, forcing a breathless wind through the tunnels ahead of it. It had filled her prison with all the signs of its passing, and then it had left her alone again. Alone, but with the hopeless certainty that the train and all its passengers was oblivious to her presence. They knew no more where Adda-Leigh was than she did herself. She was in darkness. Total darkness.

LIKE THE BUMBLEBEE

Sam sat on his haunches on the beach. His feet sank into the cold sand. Fat, grey-bellied flies hopped around his ankles. At his back, a bank of crumbling earth rose over him. Dry grass maintained a meaningless whispering while dusty ox-eye daisies nodded their heads in mindless assent.

A coarse brown blanket was draped around Sam's hunched shoulders, and an orange bath towel was wrapped around his waist. The towel was fastened with a bulldog clip to form an improvised kilt. Six months ago his skin had been a sallow gold colour, a pleasing enough blend inherited from his Oriental mother and his Welsh father. Like both of his parents his hair had been jet-black.

Now he was transformed. Although he was still

basically humanoid in form, his body had undergone some alarming alterations. His hair had coarsened and thickened into jagged quills. His skin had blistered and peeled and hardened until he was covered in knots, calluses and scaly protuberances. His enlarged jaw jutted forward and his teeth were needle sharp.

This shocking metamorphosis had already begun when he first met Father David. And still it was not complete. The course these changes took was erratic and inconsistent. At times the pain it caused him was intense. He would wake in the night tearing at his flesh with clawed fingers, screaming out, 'Why? Why is this happening to me?'

And Father David, roused from his armchair by the cries, would answer, serious-faced, 'Growing pains. It is just your age.' But Sam refused to see the funny side.

His skin tone varied in colour from bruise-blue to screaming rust-orange. The blanket and towel weren't really necessary. His hide was so bloated and thickened that, like a crocodile or iguana or rhinoceros, he did not appear naked even without a stitch of clothing. Nevertheless, there were still times when Sam could not bear to go without a covering of some kind. He clung desperately to his old life, to his former human-ity. And so he draped himself in cloths and wound a towel around his waist. But it only took a day or two before contact with the rough scales of his body surface would wear the fabric to rags.

There had been two mirrors in the cottage when they'd first arrived in Ireland. Sam smashed them both to pieces. Looking at his reflection was unbearable. Fourteen years bad luck, he had told himself, miserably. One for every year of his life.

After the fire had destroyed his home back in London, Sam had felt terribly alone. He'd sought out Father David, the only person that seemed to understand anything about the changes he was enduring. Now, he wondered if he'd made the right decision.

Far out to sea, Sam was aware of the terns and the gulls, and a lone gannet, all dive-bombing the fish in the bay. In front of him, the beach was strewn with sea-washed debris. Bleached plastic bottles, salt-whitened shards of timber, coils of tar-blackened nylon rope. Not far from where he sat, a cloud of flies buzzed over the sunken, deflated body of a drowned chicken. A faded blue toothbrush lay next to it, half-buried in the sand.

Sam didn't have to look at these things to know they were there. His sense of smell, his hearing, his sense of touch were all just as sensitive, just as perceptive, as his vision, which in itself was far more powerful than any human's eyesight. These changes had come alongside the dramatic physical transformation.

A sixth sense had developed too. His gifts of telepathy seemed to have no limits. Already, he had discovered how to convert his thought waves into signals he could patch into the mobile phone network. He could track down people he knew well, simply by sensing their presence and homing in on that sensation. And he could identify intentions in others, particularly violent intentions. He was sure he could hone those skills into genuine mind-reading ability given practice. But he was still learning to control and understand his gifts. Progress was slow. Sometimes he seemed to be going backwards.

There was no one on the beach. There was no one for miles around. The farmer whose fields bordered the shoreline at Ballylach had driven into town an hour earlier. Sam had smelt the petrol fumes and heard the roar of the car engine, even though the farmhouse was five miles away. The farmer was their closest neighbour. Sam could be sure he was alone.

Just to be certain, he closed his eyes and reached out with his mind to check on Father David. He intruded only close enough to know that the priest was asleep in his armchair, in the grey-stone cottage up on the headland. The strain of acting as Sam's one-to-one tutor, twenty-four hours a day, was exhausting the small priest. He spent a lot of time asleep.

It was five months since Sam had first met Father

David but he knew now that the priest had spent years searching for him. It was he who'd made Sam understand that he was probably the very last of the dragon-folk of Luhngdou. Father David was also of Luhngdonese descent, though, like most Luhngdonese, he lacked the dragon gene. He was the nearest thing Sam had to a living relative from his mother's side of the family.

The boy stood up and let the blanket fall. It caught on the leathery growths that disfigured his back. He shook his shoulders and the blanket crumpled into the sand. Flies hopped away in all directions, fleeing in panic.

Sam flexed his cramped muscles. The wings he kept folded into his back now unfurled, painfully. He stretched his wingtips to their fullest extent, feeling the wind catch and tug, resisting, buoying him up. He leaned forward and pushed himself off the ground. His shadow passed across the sand.

'Aerodynamically impossible, of course,' Father David had said, when he'd tried coaching Sam in flying techniques in the field behind the cottage. 'Like the bumblebee.'

Sam had refused to do any flight training for the past three weeks.

'I'm not a performing parrot!' he'd said, spitting an angry globule of fire into a patch of thistles, which burst into flames. 'I'm not doing it any more!'

'Instinct will only get you so far.'

'I said, I'm not doing it any more.' Sam had stomped away, his long, clawed toes tearing at the grass, defiantly pedestrian.

But the muscles in his back and shoulders, and in the cramped wings themselves, now ached to be put to use. He was glad the priest couldn't see him gliding over the rock pools like some gigantic prehistoric bird.

Sam came to rest on a flat patch of hard-packed sand, left smooth by the rolling of the tide. He extended the index finger on his right hand. Knob-knuckled and elongated, but with an alien grace to their articulation that Sam, in spite of himself, was almost proud of, his fingers were each tipped with an elegantly curved talon.

Delicately, he scored the sand, swiftly executing a stylised line drawing of a girl's face. Large long-lashed eyes and high cheekbones. He had perfected a likeness that worked to his own satisfaction, though it was, in truth, a rather idealised portrait.

But Sam didn't dare try to contact Adda-Leigh, either through telepathy or more conventional methods. He had last seen her in London. And she had seen him. A naked flying freak tapping at her window in the early hours of dawn. The memory of that last parting haunted him.

It had seemed the right thing to do at the time, to say goodbye. But now he felt ashamed of his feelings for her, which had bloomed over the months he'd spent in Ireland into full-blown obsession. He thought about her all the time, but how could she ever think of him without a shiver of revulsion? He prayed that she'd put that morning's vision down to a particularly vivid nightmare, and that she thought no more of it, while at heart he also hoped, fervently, that she hadn't completely forgotten him.

Establishing contact with her via the mobile phone network might be possible, but the distance would mean extra effort. He would have to build up his psychic stamina. He used that difficulty as an excuse to himself for not even attempting to contact her. In truth, he was afraid of how she would react if she knew he was trying to keep in touch. The fear of rejection chilled him to the bone.

So instead of talking to Adda-Leigh he spent hours plucking radio transmissions out of the ether, seeking out those music stations that played the most mournful ballads and the most doom-laden rock songs he could find. He drew pictures of Adda-Leigh in the sand, close to the sea. Then he watched as the waves rolled in and washed away her image, leaving nothing behind but the smooth wet sand.

INVOLVEMENT IN THE BALKANS

Father David lay in his armchair, floundering in the shallows of sleep. His eyelids flickered. He turned his head. His mouth opened in a muffled cry, but he did not wake. He was dreaming of the past . . .

BOSNIA-HERZEGOVINA – 1993

The armoured personnel carrier lurched forward, moving across the bridge. A sniper's bullet ricocheted off the side plating with a terrible clang.

'I say! Someone's not happy!' The Major leaned forward, his eyes twinkling amidst a veritable Nile delta of laughter lines.

The Major has smiled this careless smile a million times before, Father David thought, in places just as dangerous as this, probably more so.

'Now listen here, young Padre,' the Major's smile deepened, 'you do realise – if things get wobbly – the UN, the British government, the army, everyone will deny all knowledge of you and yours?' He chuckled, a deep and fruity laugh, edged with a wheezy hoarseness that came of smoking too many cheroots in the officer's mess. 'Won't be lying, either. They don't know you're here. This mission – strictly personal. My decision. My risk.'

'Thank you.' Father David swallowed, the harsh taste of bile in his throat. The taste of fear. Would he fail in this, his very first mission as an agent of the Companions? Would he and his bodyguard even make it to the fortress alive?

The carrier jolted, rearing over something on the track. The bridge was behind them now. They were in hostile territory. The priest's helmet slipped down over his eyes. He pushed it up again with a sweaty hand.

'Thanks not required.' The Major smiled. 'Your father – my father – both fought in Korea.'

Father David looked at the Major.

'But they fought on opposing sides.'

The Major shrugged and grinned. He clapped Father David on the shoulder.

'Who cares? Both fellow soldiers! Anyway, there

are no bloody sides!' He exploded into another throaty laugh. 'Never are. Not really. Here in the Balkans – good case in point. Bloody chaos! Everyone fighting everyone else. You'll see. Old military adage: "Never march on Moscow, don't eat yellow snow, and avoid involvement in the Balkans!" Whoops – too late!'

Another gale of laughter from the Major. He then put on an expression of mock seriousness.

'One question though, Padre . . .' He pointed to Mrs Hare, who was sitting opposite the two men, her eyes closed, her automatic rifle cradled in her arms, a dark green beret covering her short greying hair. 'Why bring your auntie along?' The Major exploded once again into wheezing merriment. Mrs Hare kept her eyes resolutely closed.

'Why bring Mrs Hare?' Now it was Father David's turn to smile, though his smile was a grim one. 'You'll see,' he said.

ABANDONED AIR

Early morning by the stables under the flyover. The last of the horses were being loaded into their trailers, soon to be driven away. The doors to the indoor arena, housed beneath the motorway itself, had been left wide open. Already the premises had a derelict, abandoned air to them. The office, the tack room, the stores, and the yard, all had been stripped of fixtures and fittings and now lay empty.

Georgette stood at a distance, alone. She was dressed in her school uniform, her bag heavy on her shoulder. She would be late. It was already after nine o'clock. But these days, being late for school no longer felt like the heinous crime she had once thought it. This was the last time she would see Dandelion.

She watched them lead him out to the trailer. She

saw him twitch his nostrils, drinking in warm summer air, and she hoped he may have recognised her scent and registered her presence amongst the sweet grass and blooming clover.

This was the spot. This place, where she was standing now. This was where, five months before, she had seen the creature towering over Adda-Leigh. This was where she had ridden Dandelion out to fight it. She had seen it stagger and belch flames. And she had seen it fly.

Adda-Leigh's story was different. The thing had saved her life, she said. It had thrown Crisp, the gun-wielding psycho, into the canal. And, she said, she had recognised it. Adda-Leigh believed the creature was Sam Lim-Evans. It was the eyes, she said.

Georgette didn't know what she believed. She had talked it through, over and over, with Adda-Leigh. They had relived that night together on countless occasions. They had argued, wept, become reconciled, vowed not to talk about it any more, but it always came up again. The horrors and mysteries of that night on the marsh would bind them together for ever. With Adda-Leigh missing, Georgette, too, felt lost.

Standing on the edge of the marsh, she watched, dully, as the trailer doors were closed on Dandelion and he was driven away.

HIM

Another train had passed by, but now there was a different sound from beyond the door. An echoing clatter. Someone climbing a flight of steps. Footsteps on the gritty stairs. Footsteps in the passageway behind the door.

Adda-Leigh held her breath, waiting, her eyes straining uselessly in the pitch-black. Her throat felt bone-dry and the back of her neck prickled with fear. It was him.

NOWHERE TO GO

Father David sighed, but his face remained expression-less. He stood in the darkened back room of the cottage, a full carrier-bag held in each hand. Their weekly supply of food had just been delivered.

When they had first arrived at the cottage, Father David had arranged for a driver from the nearest town to pick up a weekly order from the supermarket, together with a canister of bottled gas, when neces-sary. The delivery-man drove the twenty miles of winding country roads out to Ballylach. Today, as usual, the driver, a rotund man with a ruddy complex-ion and a salt-and-pepper moustache, craned his neck, trying to look past the small priest standing at the door. Sam kept to his room, out of sight.

Father David remained in the cottage doorway until

the man drove away, then carrying two of the half-dozen bulging shopping bags that were piled around the front step he went inside. 'I expect he thinks I'm keeping a scarlet woman hidden away in the house,' he called to Sam.

'He obviously doesn't know how boring you really are,' said Sam. He lay on the floor. Behind him, the bed, tipped on its side, was leaning against the wall. A soot-blackened bedspread had been nailed over the window. A scorched mattress, its bent springs jutting through tears in the charred fabric, lay sagging against the wall, next to the bed frame. Sam's attempts at sleeping in this bed, when they'd first come to the cottage, had ended in near disaster.

Father David sighed again. 'Help me put away the food, please,' he said. He carried the bulging carrier-bags back out and across the narrow hall to the kitchen.

Sam didn't move. He lay on the floor, one hand supporting his head, his wings stretched out behind him, trailing in the dust that covered the bare floorboards. He closed his eyes and dipped into the radio waves beamed out from Dublin, Liverpool, London, and via satellites orbiting the earth. He picked out a crunching flurry of guitar chords, received the signal, and let the music pound through his head, setting the teeth buzzing in his jutting lower jaw. The bones in his face had grown some more lately, and his cheeks ached horribly. The music hurt him too, blitzing through his brain like a sonic headache. But he let it do its worst, pumping up the volume until he could feel nothing but the crushing beat, the wild scream of amplification, the relentless bludgeoning of the snarling vocals.

Sam was aware of Father David calling him, but he ignored it. The priest was from Luhngdou, just as Sam's mother had been. The Luhngdonese were Oriental. They looked like Chinese or Vietnamese people, but they were not. Sam knew this. He also knew that he and Father David were in all likelihood the last survivors of their race.

He did not remember his mother very clearly, but he remembered her enough for Father David's presence to remind him that he'd lost her. And, remembering his mother led him to thoughts of his father, Llew, who wasn't dead, but injured, badly burned after his booze-fuelled accident had set their home ablaze. Sam found it hard to feel much sympathy, though he knew that even now Llew was enduring skin grafts and painful treatments, somewhere just across the sea in Wales. Llew didn't know where Sam was. And Sam hadn't even tried to contact him. The life he had led with his father in their tiny London flat now seemed a remote memory. He found it impossible to imagine what he would say to Llew, if he ever saw him again.

Sam knew none of this was Father David's fault. He had come halfway around the world to help him, to guide him through the many horrors of dragon trans- formation. But still Sam took a savage delight in blam- ing the little priest for all of it.

He heaved himself to his feet and, crouching low, dipped his head beneath the doorframe and shuffled out of the bedroom, heading for the back door.

'Sam.' Father David stepped into the passageway, a packet of scouring pads in one hand and a box of Pop- Tarts in the other. 'We must put away this shopping. And then we have work to do. The schedule . . .'

'You and your schedule!' Sam's voice was deep and hoarse. His throat still itched on the inside. 'You stick to the schedule if you want,' he said, 'I'm going out.' He pushed past the small priest and flung the back door open. Sam left the cottage without a backward glance.

But he had nowhere to go. He stomped off across the empty field behind the cottage. Later he flew, but kept low, lazily dragging his clawed toes across the ground, his head down and his wings flapping with a slow, slovenly beat.

He sat beside the track up on Allen's Point, the sea at his back, pounding at the foot of the cliffs far below him. The wind whipped up grains of sand and salt and grit, hurling it against his hide. He sat so still that he became virtually invisible to all but the most sensitive of observers. A hare loped along the tarmac and paused, close by him. Sam watched the wind ruffle its fur, heard the beating of its heart and sensed the warmth and richness of the blood in its veins. It had no idea he was there.

Sam was still in the grip of an indolent trance, silent and unseen, when the four teenagers from Cullithin rode by on their pushbikes. Though the place they stopped to rest, and to pass round a frothing bottle of pink lemonade, was a good half-a-mile further along the road, Sam heard every word they said. That was when he decided that he, too, would attend the village fête at Cullithin.

POPPIES IN THE SNOW

Father David put away the groceries. He stocked the freezer with microwave pizzas and bags of oven chips, which were among the few things he could persuade Sam to eat.

The priest sighed. Sam was far from being a model student. And yet Father David was committed to tutoring him in the ways of the dragon-folk. Sam needed to learn to control his faculties if his ever-increasing powers weren't to drive him insane.

And the priest was also uncomfortably aware that Sam needed to learn to protect himself. The Order of the Knights of the Pursuing Flame, a secret organisation devoted to the extermination of the dragon-folk, had been defeated over a decade before by the Companions, a group set up to oppose the cruelties of the

Order. And yet the danger didn't seem to have passed. Father David had once belonged to the Companions. He'd grown up amongst them and had taken holy orders under their tutelage. But he'd broken from them before beginning his search for Sam. He now knew that someone had followed him to the marsh where he'd found the last of the dragon-folk. Someone had set that half-mad racist Crisp on them and enabled him to murder Mrs Hare. The priest knew that the Companions had become corrupted, the viciousness of their centuries old war with the Order had seen to that. Now he couldn't be sure whether it was his old enemy the Order who had been behind Mrs Hare's death, or their former friends the Companions. Cold from the freezer numbed his hands. His dream the night before had awoken old memories. Now, the chill in his fingers reminded him again of the Balkans, a decade earlier. As he stacked all the food and the various household products away in the appropriate cupboards, working methodically, mindlessly, his thoughts were elsewhere. He was in Bosnia once more.

BOSNIA-HERZEGOVINA – 1993

Heavy machine-gun fire tore the heart out of the morning. Then an explosion so loud that Father David was made temporarily deaf. The impact of the blast threw him roughly against the armour-plated sides of the personnel carrier.

He looked around, dazed. The world had been plunged into an unnatural silence. He had the impression that everything was happening in slow motion. Mrs Hare adjusting her spectacles seemed to take for ever. But then he was suddenly aware that the interior of their armoured vehicle had filled with smoke.

'Time we were elsewhere, chaps!' The Major's voice betrayed no emotion. He sounded distant, muffled. But, at least, thought Father David, I can hear again. The young priest made no move to leave the stricken vehicle, however. The shock of the explosion had left him weak.

Mrs Hare grabbed him by the sleeve and led him out into the fierce cold of the snow-covered landscape. He looked back and saw the armoured vehicle was burning fiercely. Black smoke belched from the cab. He felt sick. What had happened to the driver?

They were on a wooded slope. Bullets cut into the trees around them, scything into branches, whining through the frozen air. Father David stumbled in a snowdrift and sat down heavily. He was in a daze. Mrs Hare gently pushed him down into the snow.

'Best get some cover, Father. Someone's taken out the APC, with a rifle grenade I think. A lucky shot. Whoever fired it will be waiting for his friends to arrive. They'll be here in a minute, then they'll move in to try and finish us off.'

'Is it them? Is it soldiers of the Order? Or have we just stumbled into the middle of the civil war?' Father David was surprised he sounded so calm and lucid. He felt anything but.

'Oh yes,' said Mrs Hare, 'it's them all right. Their fortress is just over that ridge. This is their perimeter patrol we've run into. They don't want us to get there, do they?'

The Major crouched next to them, breathing in jagged gasps. He was clutching at a wound to his forearm, holding it tightly, applying pressure in an effort to staunch the bleeding. Drops of blood fell into the snow. Father David watched them spread through the icy crystals, each drop blooming like a flower filmed on a time-lapse. Poppies in the snow.

'Blast!' the Major said. He clenched his teeth. 'This could be ruddy awkward!'

But Mrs Hare was scrambling up the slope. She glanced down at them, briefly, as she neared the crest. 'You two stay down here. I shan't be long.' Her spectacles had slipped down her nose. She pushed them back into place, took a firm grip on her assault rifle, and disappeared into the snow-filled landscape beyond the slope.

'Where the devil does she think she's going?' said

the Major.

'The Order has a squad of infantrymen closing in on us. I imagine she's getting herself into a good position to hit them in the flank before they get here.'

'Good grief! Who exactly is she?' The Major looked bewildered, still clutching at his wounded arm.

'Prudence Hare. Mrs Hare to you and I, Major.' The frozen air and banked-up snow cleared Father David's mind. Mrs Hare was doing her job. He felt a strange sense of relief. He had nothing to do now but wait. 'Mrs Hare was washed ashore on Luhngdou Island in the South China Sea when she was around nine years of age,' he told the Major. 'No one knows how she came to be in the sea, nor how she survived in those shark-infested waters. She had clearly been well brought up, probably the daughter of English ex-patriots living in the Far East, and she's never lost her accent or her fondness for certain English foods. But her memory of everything prior to hitting the shores of Luhngdou is entirely erased. She grew up among the agents of the Companions; her late husband was a high ranking member of the organisation, killed on active service. She has been highly trained in martial arts and all forms of combat.' Father David shivered. 'I'm sorry to say, when it comes to violence, she's a natural. But then, she may well save our lives.'

From beyond the ridge came the sound of gunfire.

The noise intensified for a while. Then there were some muffled explosions. Then silence. A bird sang, somewhere in the frozen woods. No gunmen arrived at the top of the slope.

'I say!' said the Major. 'Your old aunt, eh? I think she's dealt with that patrol!'

Father David simply nodded.

'I say!' breathed the Major, once again, and there was awe in his voice, as well as relief.

THE DEEP

'Please,' said Adda-Leigh, 'I need light.'

She had heard the scrape of the grill in the door being slid open. She could smell the tray of warm food that had been pushed into her cell. But she could see nothing.

The footsteps hesitated outside the door. There was a long silence. She sat in the darkness, her heart pounding. She prayed silently that he wouldn't unlock the door. That he wouldn't come into her cell.

This was the first time she had spoken to her captor since she'd found herself a prisoner, she didn't know how long ago. The events of the kidnap were a blur. A bag forced over her head. Rough hands bundling her into the boot of a car. A nightmare drive through darkness leading to incarceration in a cell with no light.

The room had clearly been prepared for her. What was once perhaps a workman's washroom and office had been converted into a prison, the door fitted with a sliding grill and reinforced with sheet steel. She'd had the impression there was more than one person present when she was taken, but here, guarding her, she was convinced there was only one. But she hadn't set eyes on him, or heard his voice. Until now.

When he spoke it was little more than a whisper. There was a trace of an accent, or a mixture of accents that Adda-Leigh couldn't quite identify.

'Darkness', he said, 'was upon the face of the deep.' The voice was low and quiet in tone, but it was not a gentle voice. There was a tremor in that whispered biblical quotation that spoke of a lifetime of torment. It was a voice wracked with pain. Adda-Leigh sat in the dark and listened, breathless with fear.

Up to now, when he'd brought her food she'd always hidden in the back of her cell, in the tiny washroom, hunched between the sink and the toilet bowl, as far from the door as she could get.

But the darkness had begun to work on her imagination. Terrifying thoughts about what might be there in the cell with her had stopped her from moving around in the pitch-black. She imagined nameless horrors lying unseen all around. Fear of what she might discover, or of what might discover her, kept her in one place. So now she was desperate for light.

The silence lengthened. She began to wonder if her captor had crept away down the stairs without making a sound and that she was alone in the dark again.

But then there was the rattle and clatter of something being pushed through the grill in the door. The sound was so sudden and so unexpected that Adda-Leigh couldn't help but cry out. She stifled the scream at once, stuffing her fist into her mouth. She remembered how she'd called out for help when she'd first found herself a captive, and how he had pounded on the door, threateningly, insistently, until she had fallen into the frightened silence she had maintained ever since. She did not wish to antagonise the man that held her prisoner. His power over her seemed to be absolute.

He spoke again. 'Let there be light,' he said softly, 'and there was light.'

Adda-Leigh listened to his footsteps descending the echoing staircase. He was gone. She reached out her hand and felt her way over the concrete floor, leaning forward towards the door, where her food awaited her, along with whatever else her captor had left behind. Her questing fingertips located a hard plastic cylinder. She gripped it, picked it up, and knew then that it was a torch.

CROSS THAT BRIDGE

The police had interviewed Georgette when Adda-Leigh went missing. They'd asked a lot of questions about Sam.

Sam had been missing for months now. No evidence of foul play had ever been found. When WPC Johns spoke to Georgette she'd made it fairly clear the police considered Sam to be just another teenage runaway. His background suggested he might have had his reasons for leaving home. Mother dead when he was seven, father a wheelchair-bound alcoholic who, since his son's disappearance, had been badly burned in a house fire and had now moved out to Wales.

Sam had run off, then, to take his chances on the streets, or in a squat somewhere in the centre of London. And now, the policewoman was suggesting, Adda-Leigh had joined him.

'But she wasn't even his girlfriend! They hadn't known each other long.' Georgette knew there was more to the disappearance than this.

'But she did like him, didn't she?' said the officer, leaning back in her chair and taking a sip from one of the two mugs of Bovril she'd made during the interview. The portable kettle sat, still wheezing and puffing out steam, on the desk in front of her.

'Well, yes. I suppose so.' Georgette bit her lip. 'But why would she just run off with him, without telling her mum and dad? Without telling anyone?' Without telling me, Georgette thought.

'Young love!' said the policewoman. 'It does funny things to the brain. Besides, there was all that business back in February. Adda-Leigh nearly got herself shot, out on the marshes. I reckon she's got a touch of post-traumatic stress disorder, the poor thing. No wonder she's decided to do a runner with young Mr Lim-Evans!'

'I was there too,' Georgette said quietly. 'I was there that night on the marsh.'

The policewoman looked at her, her eyebrows puckered. 'It's just a theory. If I'm right she'll soon get tired of living rough with Sam and she'll be back home in no time.'

'And if you're wrong?' Georgette's question hung on the air.

WPC Johns looked away. 'Let's cross that bridge if we come to it.' She sounded uncertain.

When she spoke again it was with a forced lightness of tone. 'Drink up your Bovril before it gets cold,' she said. 'Full of beefy goodness, that is!'

BLIND

Sam insisted on a rigorous and lengthy session of psychic training that evening. Father David was delighted. As a student, Sam had been a serious disappointment to the small priest. Now, out of the blue, he was actually requesting tuition.

Father David hadn't liked to bring the training session to a close until Sam himself declared he had had enough. They carried on into the small hours. The priest finally stumbled into his chair in the living room and succumbed to exhausted sleep. He was drained in both mind and body from the rigours of teaching a skill he could never hope to possess himself.

Sam was aware of the priest, curled up in his chair. The small man slept, dreaming, it seemed, of snow and blood. Sam's mind picked up a sense of the dream as half-formed jumbled images and sensations. Dreams, unconscious thoughts and strong emotions were always easy to pick up. Once, when his father had been in great danger, Sam had somehow established a clear telepathic link, a moment of crystal-clear second sight in which he saw plainly the peril his father was in. He'd not been able to manage anything like it since, despite all the psychic training sessions Father David could devise. If Sam had wanted to build up his mind-reading skills, dreams were one of the few possible starting points currently open to him. But he felt no curiosity about Father David's dream. He closed the bedroom door and began his preparations.

He'd found the hooded raincoat in the back of the shed beside the cottage. He dragged it out from behind his mattress. A crop of dusty mould was growing on the oilskin fabric. Sam breathed gently on it, incinerating the mould but inadvertently scorching the cloth here and there. A rank smell arose from the heated waterproof.

Whoever had originally owned the coat must have been a big man. Had Father David worn it he would have been swamped. The hem would have trailed on the ground and the hood would have completely covered his head. On Sam it was a tight fit. The coat fell to just above his knees.

Sam wrapped a scarf around his neck, pulling it up

so it covered his jutting lower jaw. He eased the oilskin hood over the spines that crowned his head and tugged it down over his brows. He wrapped his feet and legs, up to the knee, in strips of bedding, tying the trailing ends and tucking them out of sight as best he could. He told himself he looked unremarkable. He told himself he would blend in at the village. His loneliness had made him blind to the truth. He knew Father David would talk him out of going if he'd asked his permission. Deep down, Sam realised the priest would be right to do so. But just now, he wasn't interested in what was right. It was already light outside. He'd go now, before there was any chance of a discussion. Leaving Father David asleep in his chair, Sam set off across the fields to Cullithin.

BAD RUBBISH

BOSNIA-HERZEGOVINA – 1993

Father David bound the Major's wound, using a field-dressing kit he'd found in the soldier's backpack.

'Thank you, Padre,' the Major said. 'Now then, I suggest you perform a bit of stealthy reconnaissance. It appears that Mrs Hare may have succeeded in securing the area, but we'd better make sure. And what the blazes has happened to the helicopter strike? They should have hit the target well before we got here.'

Father David looked at the Major.

'You seem to be very well informed about our business, Major? I thought you were simply acting as our guide?'

'Yes, well . . .' the Major said grinning. 'Operate on

need to know basis, and all that. Truth is, as well as being a bona fide Special Forces bod, I'm also one of your lot. A mole.'

Father David said nothing.

'I'm an agent of the Companions,' said the Major. 'Just like you and Mrs Hare, except I'm a more recent recruit. My orders were to deliver you two to the target area to rendezvous with Operation Command. They're the ones with the heavy ordinance, who're supposed to take out the fortress and any patrols that might have been sent out. So they may be surprised to find Mrs Hare has beaten them to the punch.'

Father David climbed the ridge and dropped low as he neared the top. From the slope below he heard the Major laugh and call out. 'Well done, lad. Perfect use of cover. We'll make a soldier of you yet!'

Looking out across a barren, snow covered plateau, Father David saw Mrs Hare waving at him. She was standing close to the stone gatehouse of the old fortress. Her prisoners were sitting in the snow in front of her, hands on their heads and their eyes on the ground. Five men in military fatigues.

'They didn't put up much of a fight,' she said, when the small priest reached her. There was a note of disappointment in her voice. 'They're mercenaries. I don't imagine they're that well paid either, considering the little amount of resistance they bothered to show. If this is the best the Order can do to protect their so-called secret HQ then they really must be down on their luck. I must admit, I don't understand it. I thought this was going to be the site of a desperate last stand.'

'I believe they were relying on the chaotic civil war in this unfortunate region to keep us at bay,' said Father David. 'They have underestimated the resources available to the Companions. And perhaps, as you say, they're down on their luck.'

He looked up at the gaunt stone ramparts of the castle. Above the gate the symbols of the Order had been carved in stone. A sword, a flaming brand, a cross, and a writhing dragon transfixed by a lance.

'This place must be close to eight hundred years old. The Order would have built it during one of their Balkan crusades, back in the thirteenth century. It seems their time is coming to an end at last.'

'Good riddance', Mrs Hare said, 'to bad rubbish! But what I don't understand is, why haven't they posted any guards on the walls, or in the gatehouse or anywhere? I've checked the fortress. It's deserted.'

'I've heard they built a network of tunnels down in the catacombs.' Father David shivered. 'Perhaps they're waiting for us down there.'

The sound of helicopter blades cut through the cold air.

'Here come the cavalry!' Mrs Hare grinned. 'I can't

wait to see their faces when they find me and my prisoners.'

A single helicopter appeared from below the tree line. It hovered over the gatehouse. The whirring blades whipped the snow up into eddying flurries.

Out of the belly of the helicopter gunship, a black-clad figure descended on a swaying rope ladder. He jumped the last three metres, performed a perfect parachute roll and ran over to Father David and Mrs Hare. The newcomer's face was hidden beneath a balaclava and a pair of snow goggles. He pushed the goggles up onto his forehead as he marched across the snow, revealing a pair of piercing, silvery-blue eyes. A light machine-gun was cradled in his arms. He pointed the weapon at Mrs Hare.

'Agent Hare. Move away. Now!' He turned to the priest. 'You too, Father. Fall back to the top of the ridge immediately.'

'My prisoners . . .' Mrs Hare began.

'Never mind them. I'll make sure things get cleaned up,' the pale-eyed man interrupted, speaking with the air of someone who expected total obedience at all times.

Mrs Hare and Father David did as they were told. They had just reached the trees when the first explosion shook the ground beneath their feet. The helicopter circled above the fortress, firing rocket after rocket into its ancient stones while they watched in stunned silence. The man in black had also retreated into the trees and was directing the attack via a walkie-talkie, which he was holding pressed against one ear.

Across the plain the fortress was being systematically destroyed. The moss-covered walls buckled and fell, heaved into devastation by earth-shaking explosions.

'My God,' said Father David, when a momentary pause in the destruction left him able to make himself heard. He realised now what the man had meant by 'cleaned up'. 'Your prisoners, Mrs Hare. They were still in the fortress. The Companions have killed them. We've killed them!'

PALE AS THE MOON

There was nothing in Adda-Leigh's cell that she didn't already know about. She swept the beam of the torch over every inch of every dusty surface. She was in a concrete box, buried somewhere, under the ground. There was just a toilet and a washbasin at the back of the room. On the bare floor, along one wall, a mattress had been laid out. This was where she slept. When her captor brought her food, she ate it sitting cross-legged on the floor.

'What do you want with me? Why have I been taken? Where is this place?' Adda-Leigh would call out her questions when her food arrived, but she received no word of reply.

The air she breathed was thick and tepid and was regularly stirred into dust-filled gales by the tube trains that rumbled by, somewhere below her. She used the torch sparingly, to conserve the batteries. But she kept it on whenever her food was delivered, to show that she appreciated the gift.

By its pale yellow beam, she caught a glimpse of her captor's hand as he passed her tray through the grill in the door. It was a large, bony hand, thin-fingered, but giving an impression of great strength, as if each finger were coiled with muscle, like the body of a small but vigorous snake. He had no fingernails. His skin was as pale as the moon.

THE ARROW

Sam waited in the woods beyond the village. He watched as preparations for the day's events got underway. Stalls were laid out on trestle tables on the grass by the river. Tables and chairs were brought from the pub and arranged in a row along the pavement in the main street. A drum kit, amplifiers and microphones were set up under a plastic awning. A string of bunting made from strips of coloured cellophane was strung across the road and twisted around the telegraph poles.

By midday, crowds of people had begun to throng the main street. There were plenty of young children, but there were also teenagers, adults, old people, the whole population of the village. There was an air of indulgent anticipation, as people looked forward to a familiar sequence of events that they had all known since childhood.

But then Curlytop arrived. His presence brought a sharp, sour flavour with it. Sam was suddenly uncomfortably aware, before he even picked the newcomer out in the crowd, that there was now someone in the village who enjoyed inflicting pain on others. When he saw the youth with the corkscrew hair he made a note to steer well clear of him. Curlytop slouched along the road that sloped down towards the river. A group of smaller youths were gathered about him. Sam could read their emotions, a mixture of fear and excitement and desperation. All of them, even Curlytop himself, were gnawed at by a hunger to fit in, to be part of a gang rather than a loner. To be one of the hunters, rather than one of the hunted. They strutted around their leader, both flinching from, and basking in, the cruel light of his sneering gaze. Curlytop was the name Sam gave him. A deliberately soppy nickname for a rather frightening individual. He never got to know his real name.

The day's programme of events got under way. A band played country and western ballads outside the pub. A tug-of-war competition started on the river-front grass. People were milling about, enjoying the sunshine, drinking mugs of tea or pints of Murphys stout.

Sam seized the moment. He would stay in the village for an hour at the most, he told himself. Keep in the background. Don't speak to anyone; don't try to buy anything, or to join in. Just watch and enjoy. Be part of a crowd of ordinary people again, if only for a little while. It crossed his mind that a year ago he wouldn't have even considered going anywhere near a village fête. Now, he was drawn to this event with a poignant yearning he couldn't resist. He walked out of the woods, keeping his knees bent and lowering his head, trying desperately to look less gigantic.

But as soon as he left the shelter of the trees he felt horribly exposed. When he joined the stream of people crossing the bridge across the river he wondered if he'd made a terrible mistake. His crouching walk and lowered head gave him a wild, lurching gait. He couldn't have been more obvious if he'd tried. Curious glances bored into him.

A little girl, crossing the bridge with her father, stared up at Sam with a look of disgust and horror. She tugged at her father's hand. 'Daddy! Look at that man!'

The girl's father glanced round at Sam, looked away, and then quickened his pace, almost pulling the child off her feet.

Keeping his eyes fixed ahead, Sam made his way towards the grassy riverbank where the tug-of-war was being held. If he could lose himself in the thick of the crowd perhaps all these burning eyes following his every lumbering step would fade away.

But, as he made his way across the pavement and onto the grass, he looked up towards the pub. He caught the fixed gaze of the one person in the village he had hoped to avoid. Curlytop was looking at him. Sam saw him nudge his companions and slowly lift his arm and point, one stubby finger jabbing the air. The finger was an arrow, aimed straight at Sam.

Back in the cottage near the sea, Father David shifted in his chair but didn't wake. He remained in the grip of his dreams, reliving the past. With Mrs Hare, he stared again at the wall of fire and the billowing plumes of black smoke, blotting out the Balkan sky. Against the curtain of flame that engulfed the old fortress, a black-clad figure carrying a machine-gun, the man with the silver-blue eyes, was walking towards them.

NUT

Georgette walked out through the school gates. No one was around. She'd been given a half-hour detention for lateness and now she was heading home, her mind still filled with melancholy calm; a quiet mood brought on by the solemn silence of the duty room.

The Head had written to her father a week ago. Georgette had seen the letter. It was unopened, propped up on the mantelpiece in the kitchen. The manila envelope and typed name and address probably looked a little too much like a demand for payment. Her dad hadn't read it yet.

Georgette knew what the letter would say. Since February her grades had fallen and instances of lateness had increased. Since the night she'd witnessed a murder on the marsh and seen Adda-Leigh saved by something inhuman, something with wings and claws and breath of fire. And now Adda-Leigh was missing. For Georgette, school had become very low priority indeed.

Mill Avenue was quiet. She had missed the usual after-school crowds of grey-clad students spilling over the pavements, streaming away in all directions. Today, it seemed, she was the last of the stragglers. Most of her fellow Marshside students would be at home by now.

As she walked past the playing fields on Gunpowder Row, somebody called her name. She ignored it. She had little interest in anything some kid on the street might want to say to her.

But the call came again. A boy's voice, hoarse, out of breath.

'Georgette! Oi! Wait up!'

It was Aaron. She turned to see him lumbering over the grass towards her. He was struggling to control a dog on a leash, an Alsatian with strikingly white fur. The dog was pulling at the lead, its tail between its legs. The whites of its eyes were showing and it was whimpering, twisting the leash around Aaron's wrist.

'Jaws! Come on, Jaws, don't muck me about!' Aaron pleaded with the dog.

Georgette stood on the pavement and watched Aaron trying to calm the white Alsatian. 'It's the cars.

Or the road,' he said. 'Makes him nervous.' Aaron gave a helpless shrug.

Georgette stepped onto the grass and walked over to Aaron, stopping an arm's-length away from him.

'What do you want?' she asked, her voice cold. She didn't trust Aaron. On that night six months before, on the night that had become the focus of all Georgette's troubled thoughts, Adda-Leigh had persuaded Aaron to help her search the marsh. They were looking for Sam. Aaron had abandoned her in the dark, left her there to bump into that madman with a gun, to face death alone. According to Adda-Leigh, she had only escaped because the creature on the marsh intervened.

'I wanted to talk to you,' Aaron said. The leash was firmly bound around his wrist by now, and the dog was tugging frantically, trying to pull away, threatening to cut off the circulation in the boy's hand. Aaron was bent double, battling to stay on his feet. 'It's about your mate, Adda-Leigh,' he said.

The dog twisted and turned and Aaron fell to his knees with a grunt. Georgette looked down at him. 'What do you care about Adda-Leigh?'

'That's what everyone says!' Aaron turned his wrist, vainly attempting to untangle the leash. 'They all know. About when I left her out on the marsh. Now no one'll talk to me! Everyone thinks I'm a right —'

The dog reared up, straining at the leash and Aaron toppled onto his side. 'Jaws!' he wailed helplessly.

'For goodness' sake!' Georgette walked over to the dog. It tipped back its head and its liquid eyes looked imploringly into hers. There was something strangely familiar about the white-furred Alsatian.

Sprawled on the ground, his wrist firmly tied up in the twisted leash, Aaron, too, gazed up at Georgette. She hesitated. 'Will your dog bite me?'

Aaron snorted. 'He's a total wuss! He won't bite nothing! I thought I'd look a right hard man, walking around with a big old dog like this. But he's scared of everything. He just shows me up all the time!'

Georgette rolled her eyes to heaven. 'How dreadful for you!' She reached out and let the Alsatian sniff her hand.

'It is,' Aaron said.

Was it possible, Georgette wondered, that Aaron really hadn't heard the sarcasm in her voice? She stroked the dog's head. It looked up at her with an expression in its eyes that spoke of both guilt and misery. Don't be silly, Georgette told herself. He's only a dog.

But she couldn't shake the feeling that she'd seen the animal somewhere before. Unclipping the leash from the studded collar, she set the Alsatian free. He bounded away, but then crept back, his belly low to the ground. He lay on the grass, panting, watching Georgette and Aaron.

Aaron unwound the leash and rubbed the reddened skin on his wrist.

'He's not even our dog,' he said, casting a resentful glance at Jaws, who looked away, tongue lolling. 'Not really. He just turned up at our house one morning, whimpering and trembling, hiding out behind the bins. He'd probably been chased there by a cat or something.'

'What was it you wanted to say?' said Georgette. She stood with her arms folded. Aaron heaved himself up onto his feet with much puffing and panting. He reached into his pocket and pulled out a greasy packet of salted peanuts. He shook a handful into his palm.

'Nut?' he said.

Georgette gave a curt shake of the head. 'What was it you wanted to say?' she said again, louder this time.

Aaron sighed. 'It's Adda-Leigh. I dunno what happened to her, but I don't reckon the Old Bill are gonna do much about it. So I want to help. I want to help you look for her. I want to help you find Adda-Leigh.'

THE END

BOSNIA-HERZEGOVINA – 1993
0930 hours

The man with the silver-blue eyes pulled off his goggles and his black balaclava to reveal a head of golden hair.

'Sir,' said Father David, inclining his head in a bow. Next to him, Mrs Hare snapped to attention.

The young priest had never met the man before but he recognised him from photographs. He was Richard Smith, the Companions' Chief of Operations. Nervously, Father David cleared his throat.

'This is Mrs Hare, sir, my operations partner, and I'm . . .'

'At ease,' the blond man said. 'Call me Richard,

Father. We needn't stand on ceremony here, in the field. I know who you are. Both of you. I've read your files.'

Richard paced restlessly back and forth. The snow crunched and moaned beneath his combat boots. 'I won't beat around the bush, Father. You're probably wondering why I wanted you aboard for this operation. You were brought along as a witness. And to administer the last rites, symbolically speaking. It is appropriate that a priest of the Companions should be present at the death of the old Order, don't you agree? You will bear testimony. The Order of the Knights of the Pursuing Flame are no more. Our intelligence tells us they're unlikely to put up any significant resistance. Over the past few years their agents have been defecting in their droves. They're defenceless. Now for the final *coup de grâce*. I have given orders to my men. Anyone still alive in there,' Richard jerked his head towards the devastated fortress behind him, 'be they man, woman or child, will be dealt with immediately. There are to be no survivors. This is the end.'

The fortress lay in ruins. Beneath the burnt-out chapel, the crypt gave access to a maze of tunnels leading to an underground laboratory complex. Richard's men, the soldiers of the Companions, had destroyed it all by the time Father David and Mrs Hare were invited to witness the demise of the Order of the Knights of the Pursuing Flame. This place was the last bastion of the Order. It was here that they were rumoured to have been developing a weapon so powerful that it would tip the balance back in their favour and give them a chance to win the secret war they had been waging for nearly five hundred years.

But they had failed. Their walls had been breached, their laboratories put to the flame, their hired soldiers, last faithful retainers and mad scientists had all been wiped out. The Grand Master himself lay dead, in an underground chamber below the old chapel. Dressed in his heavy ceremonial robes, embroidered with the arms of the Order, he lay on his back, his sightless eyes staring at the once richly decorated ceiling, now scorched and blackened by fire.

'He took poison,' Richard said. 'Couldn't bear to look me in the eye, knowing that he'd lost everything. The old fool!' He turned on his heel and marched out of the chamber, leaving Mrs Hare and Father David alone with the dead man.

'The Order was a pitiless organisation,' said Father David. 'Hungry for power, obsessed with the extermination of an entire people, my own people. For all we know, they may well have succeeded in that aim. There may be no survivors of the dragon-folk line of Luhngdou. And, yet, for all that, I'm still sickened by this slaughter. I am ashamed to be a member of the Companions.'

Mrs Hare said nothing.

It was then that Father David saw movement, from the corner of his eye. He sensed Mrs Hare stiffen beside him. Slowly, she raised her assault rifle to her shoulder.

Father David stared at the body of the Grand Master. The thick cloak the old man wore was spread out all around him. There was movement beneath its heavy folds.

Mrs Hare took aim, her finger on the trigger of her gun.

'Wait!' Father David stepped forward. He grasped the hem of the cloak and swept it back. There, huddled against the dead man's torso, pale-skinned, naked and shivering, was a child, a small boy no more than three years old.

BURIED

Adda-Leigh listened to the hum, rattle and moan of the tube train speeding through the tunnel below. The stale wind billowed about her cell.

She had decided to try to count the days of her captivity by the number of meals her captor brought her. Three a day, she guessed. The food was always the same. Tinned fruit for breakfast. Tinned soup for lunch. Casserole or macaroni cheese for dinner. From a tin, naturally.

Since she began taking note of her mealtimes, Adda-Leigh calculated she had been a prisoner for twenty days. But time was beginning to lose its meaning for her.

Now, with the torch switched off to save the batteries, she lay on her mattress in the total darkness and, not for the first time, she began to cry silently. She felt utterly lost, abandoned and alone. She had no idea why she had been taken or what fate her abductor intended for her. It was as if she had been buried alive.

One hope burned within her. She remembered the marsh, how she had felt when the grey-haired woman had been shot, when the gunman had turned his weapon on her. She had been terribly afraid. Her life had been in danger. And somehow, Sam had known and had come to save her. Sam, her own dragon-boy. He had done it before, surely he could do so again?

'Come on, Sam,' she whispered into the darkness. 'Find me, wherever I am. I'm lost without you, boy. Come get me out of here.'

THREE ROSES

On the grass by the river, beneath the shady boughs of a cherry tree, three teenaged girls dressed in diaphanous silk dresses were presenting prizes to a selection of children who had been performing some Irish dancing for the enjoyment of the crowd. The three teenage prize-givers were wearing tiaras and sashes. They were the local beauty queens. The Rose of Cullithin and her two attendants.

Towering over the crowd, breathless and stifling under the summer sun in his scarf and hooded coat, Sam was overwhelmed by the good-natured atmosphere of the village. The girls in the sashes looked like fairy-tale princesses, more beautiful than any girls he had ever seen. Apart from Adda-Leigh, of course. But he wasn't allowing himself to think about Adda-Leigh.

Sam was among a group of his fellow human beings for the first time since leaving England. He felt suffused in a companionable glow. The prize-winning children all seemed charming, the onlookers warmhearted and kindly. He allowed himself to ignore the tingle of disquiet that was creeping over him. He told himself that Curlytop had merely pointed him out to his mates for a quiet snigger and that would be the extent of their cruelty. He blocked the scream of his extrasensory perceptions, trying to warn him of a fast approaching threat.

A band playing jigs and reels started up outside the pub. Sam turned around to look. It was only then that he saw Curlytop and his gang pushing their way through the crowd, heading straight for him.

'Freak!' Curlytop yelled at the top of his voice, lifting an arm and stabbing his finger in Sam's direction.

'Leave the poor feller alone, now!' An old man in a flat cap rounded on Curlytop, but the youth just grinned insolently into his face and pushed past him. People in the crowd tutted and glared, but the boys ignored them, their eyes fixed on their quarry.

Sam looked at the gang as they shouldered towards him like sharks closing in on a stranded swimmer. His nerve broke. All the layers of self-deception he had built up to get himself to the village crumbled away in an instant. How had he ever thought he could blend in among ordinary humans again? That single shouted syllable – Freak! – echoed around his head. He had to get away.

Sam lurched forward, the crowd falling back with a collective gasp of alarm. A rope had been strung along the perimeter of the grass to separate the crowd from the performers. Sam ploughed into this cordon and stumbled forward, heading instinctively for the river. The coat and the bound cloth on his legs felt like bonds, holding him back, tying him down and ensnaring him. He flexed the muscles in his back, shifted his trapped wings. He heard the sound of fabric tearing.

The cordon rope caught around his foot as he lurched forward. He tripped and fell to the ground, thrown down in a sprawling mass at the feet of the three teenage beauty queens. They huddled together, open mouthed with shock, their backs to the trunk of the cherry tree.

'He's attacking the girls!' Curlytop roared at the top of his voice. 'At him, lads!'

Sam struggled to his feet. The sleeve of his coat split and fell open, revealing the bare flesh of his arm from the shoulder to the elbow, puckered and distorted, in a variegated colour scheme of slate-grey and raw-orange. As one, the crowd let out an involuntary groan of shock and of horror.

Sam ran for the riverbank. He heard the Rose of Cullithin scream as he brushed past her.

'After him!' Curlytop shouted.

Sam slid on his belly down the bank and splashed into the water. The river was wide, but, to Sam's utter dismay, it was little more than ankle-deep. Flat on his stomach, he floundered in the shallows like a stranded whale, kicking and clawing at the pebble-strewn riverbed.

The first stone struck him as he dragged himself to his feet. He looked up to see Curlytop's gang spread out along the bank. They were picking up stones and hurling them down at him. A lucky shot caught Sam a glancing blow between the eyes and he staggered back, his vision all a-dance with blotches of splintered light, the water rushing round his feet.

Clawing at his eyes, Sam let out a cry of anguish and despair. He felt the cry burn in his throat and explode through his mouth and turn to a plume of fire, arcing over the water to the bank, scorching the grass. The gang of youths scattered with shouts of alarm.

Sam felt his clawed toes rip through their cloth bindings. He balanced on the balls of his feet, free now to gain a proper foothold on the slippery riverbed. He let his instincts take over and sprang forward, kicking up a great wall of spray as he made his escape.

He could still hear the clamour of the villagers as he

sped away. A group of adults had rounded up the stone-throwers and were giving them a stern talking to. Curlytop's voice was raised in self-justifying protest.

'But he was a lunatic! Did you not see? He was at us with a blowtorch!'

Sam kept to the riverbed until he could see the banks on both sides were thick with whitethorn and bramble. By now he could sense he was far away from the village, out in the fields again where no one was there to gawp, to point, to shout and throw stones.

He sprang up the bank in a single leap and went hurtling across a meadow full of sheep. The flock parted before him, running to all corners of the field, bleating with alarm. Sam didn't slow his pace until he reached the cover of the woods on the far side. He disappeared among the trees and the undergrowth, like a hunted beast seeking the cool, green sanctuary of the forest.

THE VISITOR

Crisp had a visitor. It was the only time anyone had come to see him in the secure unit where he'd been confined for the murder of Mrs Hare.

He sat in the chair, the restraints tight on his wrists. To his astonishment, the orderly left him alone in the room. But the sedatives he'd been given were powerful. He knew he didn't have a chance of escape.

The door opened. A familiar figure walked slowly into the room. Richard Smith, the man who'd got him involved in that business out in Marshside, on the night he first saw one of *them*.

He shuddered at the memory and strained against the straps on his wrists. Crisp had been a racist in his time, had belonged to a far right group who'd believed in an England for whites only. But now he'd found there was something out there more horrifying to him than a multiracial society. The alien filth, the dragon monsters, the beasts he was sure were already invading his country by stealth. That's what he'd seen on the marsh. A monster. He'd told everyone, the police, the judge and jury, the prison wardens, but they all thought he was mad. He'd ended up in this secure unit, where he spent most of his time asleep, pumped full of anti-psychotic drugs. Dragon-men swooped and roared through his every nightmare.

Richard Smith was speaking. 'Listen carefully, Crisp. I have more influence than you realise. It is within my power to arrange a spectacular administrative error here at this unit. You will be mistaken for another inmate, and you will be released. I have influence. Agents who are deep undercover. What I lack is foot soldiers. And you, my friend, are the quintessential foot soldier.'

At the word 'soldier' Crisp jerked back his head.

'You want me to fight them? The monsters? Is that it?' His voice was slurred but urgent. 'I killed the old woman, like you said. But it's the alien filth we have to fight, isn't it?'

Richard Smith raised his eyebrows. Then he chuckled briefly, a cold and humourless sound. 'I had forgotten your past allegiances. If you'd like to think of our enemies as alien filth that's quite all right by me. Only remember this. I expect total obedience. Anything less and you won't live to regret it. Now I will leave you to prepare yourself. Find a way to avoid taking your medication. When you're released make your way to where we first met. Wait for me there. I have to go away for a few days but I shall return to issue you with your orders.'

'We'll kill it! The dragon.' Crisp rocked wildly on his chair. 'We'll kill it, won't we, sir?'

'Address me as Master, if you please.' Richard Smith smiled. 'And yes, when our purpose is fulfilled, we shall kill the dragon.'

LOST AND FOUND

Georgette waited for Aaron on Mire Street. He was twenty minutes late.

'Where have you been!' she said when he finally arrived, dragging Jaws on the end of his lead. Georgette's voice was harsh and shrill. She winced at the sound of it, but she was angry and couldn't help herself. 'I've been waiting here since seven!'

'I had to finish me tea, didn't I?' Aaron said, wiping his mouth with the back of his hand.

Georgette looked at the white dog. 'You've brought Jaws.' The Alsatian cringed and cowered behind Aaron's legs as a man rode past on a bicycle. 'Is that a good idea?'

'My dad reckons he could be an ex-police dog.'

'Well, I can see why they might have chucked him out of the force.'

'Yeah, but the point is, if he went through basic training he should be able to follow a scent. Have you got anything of Adda-Leigh's?'

Georgette folded her arms. 'But he might *not* be an ex-police dog! I mean, how would your dad know?'

'He knows a lot about dogs, my dad does,' Aaron said.

Georgette pursed her lips. She looked at Jaws again. The white Alsatian was sitting on his haunches with his back bowed, looking up at her, panting sheepishly.

'The guard dog at the old stables was ex-police,' she said, doubtfully. 'He was an Alsatian too, but he was grey and brown. He ran away from the stables, in the end. He was no good. The police got rid of him after he bit the Chief Constable, apparently.'

'The only thing Jaws'll bite is his dinner,' said Aaron, gloomily. 'And even then he only nibbles at it.' He brightened up. 'But maybe he'll be an expert tracker! Let's try it! I mean, what have we got to lose?'

Ten p.m. The evening sky glowed a luminous turquoise overhead but the daylight was draining away fast. They had lost Jaws.

Georgette was hot and tired. She was also angry and scared. Aaron was lagging behind again. It was a relief, at least, to be away from his incessant running commentary on the progress, or lack of it, of their search.

They'd taken the dog to Union Road, where Adda-Leigh lived. Georgette had let Jaws sniff at a hair band Adda-Leigh had left in the kitchen at the Ferryman's Arms the last time she'd been there. Jaws had set off, seemingly with a purpose. They followed him along Glass Street, and down through the quiet back streets lined with lock-up garages and closed-down factory premises.

As they'd turned into a nameless street where a row of darkened office blocks faced a sprawling breaker's yard, Jaws had suddenly bolted. They'd been looking for him ever since.

'Jaws!' Georgette called. Her throat was sore, but she had lost any embarrassment she might have felt earlier about yelling out the dog's name in the empty streets. Despite her own unease, out in the rapidly darkening night in a deserted area of town, she was determined not to let Aaron give up the search.

The large youth lumbered up to her, breathing heavily.

'I can't go on!' he said. He gasped for breath. 'I'm cream crackered! Done in! I've had it! And it's late. My Mum'll kill me if I don't get home soon. Can't we come back and look tomorrow?'

Georgette rounded on him, furiously. 'You want to

leave your dog out here? You want to abandon him, like you did Adda-Leigh, out on the marsh? What if he's found her, in one of these old factories? You want to give up on both of them?'

Aaron winced. He held his hands up, as if to ward off a series of blows. 'All right! All right! I was just saying. I can't help it if I'm tired, can I?'

Walking on in tense silence, they turned into a shadowy side road that ran alongside the railway. Facing the tracks was a disused warehouse. The building had been gutted by fire some time ago. Charred roof beams pointed at the sky. Empty windows gazed blindly into the gathering gloom.

A train clattered by, the carriages, mostly empty, spilled light from their windows in a flickering cinematic projection, the reflections dancing jerkily across the blackened bricks of the warehouse. The train passed, and the gloomy stillness of the lifeless road reasserted itself. Georgette had the nervous sensation that someone was behind her. She glanced over her shoulder, then she spun round.

'Look!'

Jaws was quietly standing in the road behind them. He was holding something in his mouth. A weather-worn book. Georgette recognised it at once. It was Adda-Leigh's diary.

RETURN TO THE FOLD

Father David woke up, his head full of darkness and smoke. The events of the past still played themselves out in his mind's eye. He sat up and pulled back the blanket that was covering him. His back ached from sleeping in the armchair.

'Sam?' he called out.

No reply.

It had been Mrs Hare who had insisted they save the child. Though Father David had been expressing his doubts about the Companions for some while, Mrs Hare had never once agreed with him, until then. They'd been assigned as partners after Father David was received into the priesthood of the Companions and they'd trained together for the past six months. Companion priests were designated non-combatant agents and were always assigned a bodyguard to protect them in the field. Father David had found Mrs Hare to have a disturbingly sanguine attitude to violence. But that day's action, the killing of the prisoners, the order to wipe out all survivors of the Order, irrespective of age, and Richard Smith's obvious relish at the prospect, had persuaded even Mrs Hare that the Companions were no longer the honourable organisation they'd once been. When it came to action, to making a decision and taking a stand, it was his bodyguard, Mrs Hare, who had taken charge. They smuggled the child out of the ruined fortress and made their escape across country.

They left the infant at a family farm. The farmer's sons had died in the civil war and his wife was past childbearing age. Here was a foster son who could grow up on the farm, to help them in their old age. No questions would be asked. There was nothing remarkable about another orphan in the Balkans at that time.

From then on there had been no going back. Father David and Mrs Hare had broken from the Companions and set out on their lone quest. At first they had no idea if there were any survivors of the dragon-folk left alive. Even among the people of Luhngdou and their descendants the vital genetic mix had always been a rarity. Metamorphosis began at around the age of fourteen. No evidence had come to light for more than a century of anyone going through the shocking changes involved. It wasn't something that could easily be covered up. For decades both the Order and the Companions had sent out agents to scour the globe with no result. But in recent years the fighting between the two secret organisations had become intense. The search for any surviving dragon-folk had been pushed into the background.

It was this fact that gave Father David hope. Perhaps somewhere someone had survived and the gene would resurface. It was thought to be unaffected by any amount of intermarrying. The person they sought may be Luhngdonese by only the most distant of connections. It was likely they would have no idea what was happening to them when the metamorphosis began.

It seemed unlikely that more than one could have slipped through the murderous hands of the Order, who weren't above massacring whole families to ensure that none would pass on the dragon-gene. So Father David and Mrs Hare hoped to track down the last of the Luhngdonese dragon-folk. Not to kill him, as the Order would have done, nor to make him a figurehead for the ruthless pursuit of greater power, as they now feared the Companions would do. Instead, their purpose was simply to take care of him, to support him during the painful years of his transition, to provide him with some semblance of the traditional knowledge, which years of secret warfare had all but wiped out.

It had taken over a decade of painstaking detective work and genealogical research, but they had found him at last. Sam. Half-Welsh, half-Luhngdonese. Good dragon stock. But it was from his Luhngdonese mother that Sam had inherited the vital genetic ingredients, carried down through the generations, which meant that, on reaching his fourteenth year, he would begin to change, to transform, to become . . . well, what he would finally become, even Father David was not sure.

And then, just at the moment of victory, when their long search had finally come to an end, Mrs Hare had been killed, shot down by a madman on the marsh. Was that the full story? Certainly, the killer had seemed mad enough. But could he have been an assassin? Had some agent of the Order of the Knights of the Pursuing Flame escaped the inferno in Bosnia and tracked them down? Or could it have been the Companions, their former comrades in arms, who had arranged for Mrs Hare to die on the marshes of northeast London? Had they become so corrupted they would assassinate one of their own? Father David wasn't sure. All he knew was that the Companions had not disbanded after the Order had been defeated. They were still out there, secretive and powerful. And although their current purpose was unknown to him, the small priest felt sure they'd be very interested in any survivors of the dragon-folk that came to light, and that their intentions would be tainted by their newfound ruthlessness.

These thoughts spun around Father David's head as he struggled to muster the energy to stand up and stagger to the bathroom to wash the sleep from his eyes. He succeeded at last, and revived by the ice-cold water from the tap, he rapped on Sam's door.

'Hello? Are you awake?'

'Oh yes. Wide awake.' But the voice that answered from behind the door was not Sam's.

Father David felt the blood chill in his veins and his stomach turned to ice. Moving in slow motion, he reached out and turned the door handle. The door swung open. In the shadows of the darkened room, a tall figure moved. A man dressed in black stepped forward.

Father David stared. 'Richard?' he said.

'No,' the man said. 'Not any more. The Council of Companions has confirmed my new title. I am now Master of the Companions, and you should address me as such.'

The Master of the Companions took another step forward and stood in the doorway, looking down at the little priest. Father David was rooted to the spot. Fear and uncertainty drained all the strength from his body. He stared at the former Chief of Operations. The silver-blue eyes were unchanged, but the golden hair was now white as snow.

'You are a sheep that has wandered from the flock, Father David.' The voice carried with it the chill menace of absolute authority. 'And I have come to bring you back into the fold.' The Master stretched out his arms and advanced. He enfolded Father David in a stifling, inescapable embrace and the Luhngdonese priest knew no more.

II

Smokescreen

THE DUST CLOCK

Adda-Leigh was counting, her voice a whisper.

'. . . twenty-seven, twenty-eight, twenty-nine . . .'

After each count of sixty she moved the index finger of her right hand slightly, locating by touch the next piece of grit placed on the circle she had traced in the dusty floor. There were sixty pieces of grit, spaced as equally as she could make them. When her hand completed a full circuit, and she felt again the distinctive, jagged crumb of cement she had placed at twelve-o'clock, she would take one of twenty-four tiny pieces of folded up paper and place it in the centre of the circle. She had no wristwatch or any way of telling the time. This was her clock.

'. . . forty-one, forty-two, forty-three . . .'

To stay walled up in her underground cell passively

waiting for her captor to decide her eventual fate was no longer an option. Adda-Leigh had made up her mind. It was time to take action. Even if she failed, even if she made things worse, she knew she had to try. Sitting in the dark with only a run-down torch for company was slowly eating away at her. All her strength, both mental and physical, was evaporating. If she waited any longer for outside events to bring about her release, then whoever it was that finally broke down the door to her prison might find there was nothing left to rescue. She had to take the initiative, before it was too late.

Lying on her back on the dusty mattress, a mattress so thin she could feel the concrete floor pressing against her shoulders, Adda-Leigh stared up into the darkness. The torch, unlit, was grasped in her left hand. She found she had to keep it close, even if it wasn't switched on. At least it gave her the option of light, if her fears about the pitch-black all around her became unbearable.

But now she was counting, and she focused all her mind upon the task. She let the repeated cycle of numbers fill her mind, forced herself to concentrate, to keep her attention on the count. It kept the fears at bay, and allowed her to measure the passing of the moments. She needed to know when *he* would bring her next meal. And the only way to find that out was to count.

'. . . seventeen, eighteen, nineteen . . .'

When she could predict the arrival of her next meal, she decided, that would be the time to make her escape.

SANCTUARY INVADED

The stone walls of the house were still standing, but the floor and roof had been gone so long that a tree had grown in front of the tumbled remains of the hearth, its branches reaching up beyond where the beams and the thatch would once have been. The forest had closed in all around the derelict building. The shade of the trees kept the dark walls slick with damp. Ferns grew in great arching swathes, both inside and outside the ruin.

Sam stumbled in through the gaping doorway and crawled through clumps of fern, into the corner of what had once been a room. He sat with his back against the wet stones and watched the massed fronds shift before his quiet gaze. It was more than a hundred years since anyone had stayed so long in that broken-down dwelling.

He allowed his mind to empty. He became utterly still. To the creatures of the forest that passed through the old house, Sam was no more a living threat than the walled-in beech tree. His heartbeat slowed. His breathing almost ceased. His consciousness had numbed itself and he felt no pain at all.

And so he remained, for hour after hour, until a thought appeared, seemingly unbidden, forcing itself on Sam's attention. To his surprise and irritation, Sam found himself thinking of Father David. An image of the little priest pressed itself into his mind's eye, with insistent clarity. Father David seemed to be about to speak, and there was an urgency in his expression that Sam couldn't ignore.

'What? What is it?' The sound of his own voice startled Sam. He wasn't the only one to be surprised. A dog-fox bolted from the fern thicket in a wild panic. The mental picture that Sam had, of Father David leaning forward to tell him something of the utmost importance, was so strong he had found himself prompting the priest, out loud. But what it was he was about to be told, he had no idea. The image was purely visual. He could not hear a word Father David was saying.

Sam had been forced to accept changes to his every perception, to the very system of beliefs he had grown up with. And so he accepted this new and unsettling aspect of his telepathic abilities as the twitching of a developing psychic muscle. What it signified he had no idea. He had a great deal to learn. Of one thing he was sure, however. Something was about to happen.

Sam rose to his feet, with his joints clicking and his scaly skin crackling as the blood quickened once more in his veins. The clothing he had dragged onto his body to visit Cullithin had been torn away and lost in his flight from the village. He was naked now, a beast of the forest.

But the potential power of his mind was far vaster than that of any other creature in the wood. And that included the sharp and dangerous mind that he now sensed approaching him. Sam could tell that whoever was coming towards the old ruin was looking for him. He had given away his position when he stood up, when he spoke. He sensed there was little point in attempting to hide. The image of Father David slipped away, tumbling to the back of his mind, where it caught, like a child's toy, a ball or a kite lodged in the thick branches of a pine tree. Sam left it there and concentrated instead on the newcomer.

A tall man dressed in black stepped through the stone doorway.

'Hello, Sam,' the man said. 'My name is Richard.' His light-blue eyes flashed like mirrors as they sought Sam out among the ferns. 'I am to be your Master.'

DETECTIVE WORK

'Creeps me out, that place.' Aaron gave an exaggerated shiver. They walked down the steps outside Glass Street police station. 'I don't think I could stand being locked up.'

Georgette was on the point of making some remark suggesting that Aaron would be lucky to avoid falling foul of the law at some time in the future, but she stopped herself. She had to admit, without Aaron and his dog she might never have found Adda-Leigh's diary.

The police were impressed with the find, there was no doubt about it, though they'd clearly been disappointed that the diary contained no written clues. Georgette had bought Adda-Leigh the diary last Christmas. She used to carry it with her but all the pages had been left blank. Nevertheless, Georgette was sure that the police would have to start taking the investigation seriously now. A thorough search of the old warehouse where the diary had been found would be the starting point. Adda-Leigh would soon be found, safe and sound, and then some semblance of normal life could be resumed. Or so Georgette told herself over and over again.

She realised Aaron was talking, asking her a question.

'Don't you think?'

'What?'

'Don't you think it's weird? I mean, why keep a diary with nothing in it?'

'Maybe she just hadn't got around to writing anything in it yet.'

Georgette remembered giving Adda-Leigh the diary. How she'd run her long, thin fingers over the smooth cover and then leafed through the blank pages, holding the unblemished book up to her face, drinking in its newness.

'You keep a diary, then, do you?' said Aaron.

Georgette hesitated.

'You do, don't you?' Aaron smirked. 'All your little hopes and dreams locked away in a journal. I'll bet you keep it under your pillow!'

'Why don't you shut your mouth?' Georgette said fiercely. Just when she was beginning to think he wasn't so bad after all.

Aaron smirked. 'All right, all right, don't get aerated!' He whistled the jingle from a TV advert, to fill in over Georgette's angry silence, and to show he wasn't bothered by it. 'Wonder why the police couldn't come to see us, instead of us having to go to the nick?' He carried on chatting to her as if no awkwardness existed. 'They could've talked to us in the comfort of our own homes. Or after school, on the way home so they don't waste any of our precious time. You know, like they did before.'

'Before? What do you mean?' Despite her very recent decision never to talk to Aaron again, something about what he'd just said struck Georgette as curious.

'You know, after Sam went missing. That tall bloke with white hair. Special Branch detective. He was waiting for me after school, down my road. Asked me about Sam's friends and all that.'

'When was this?' Georgette had stopped and was staring at Aaron, her eyes wide.

'A month or two ago. Didn't he speak to you, too? He said he was going to.'

'What did you tell him?'

'Look, calm down! He was a detective, looking into Sam's disappearance. Showed me his ID and everything. He just asked me about Sam. About his friends and that. He kept going on about . . .' Aaron broke off abruptly. He looked back at Georgette. 'He asked me a load of questions about Adda-Leigh.'

Georgette grabbed Aaron by the arm and turned him around.

'Mind the jacket!' he said, glancing at Georgette's hand gripping his arm, her knuckles white. 'Where we going now?'

'Back to the police station. Hasn't it occurred to you that your white-haired detective may not have been a real policeman at all?'

Georgette marched briskly back up the steps to Glass Street police station, tugging a reluctant Aaron along behind her.

WHITE ROOM

Father David came to his senses in a white room. Walls and ceiling and bare floor, all were painted white. White light illuminated the room, flooding in from high windows, which were narrow and glazed in thick, frosted glass. There was the sound of the sea, close by, waves crashing on a shingle beach.

'Hello?'

He was lying on the floor, but now he sat up. There was no furniture in the room. It was completely empty. A corridor led away, through the open door. Father David was sure he'd seen a movement out in the corridor, someone retreating into the darkness beyond the painfully bright room he sat in.

'Who is there?'

There was no reply. Just the sound of waves breaking

on the shore, and the distant shriek of gulls.

He stood up a little too quickly and he staggered, light-headed. It was as if he were wading through breaking waves, with wet sand shifting under his feet. He stumbled to the door, clung onto the frame and hung there, gasping, while the dizziness passed.

'What has happened?' he said, aloud. The familiar sound of his own voice was reassuring, helping to subdue the sweeping rush of panic that threatened to engulf him. He didn't know how he came to be in the white room. The last thing he remembered was waking from a dream in his chair at the cottage.

'What is this place?' The sound of his voice died away, swallowed up in the still air of the empty room.

THE TIME

It was nearly time.

Adda-Leigh found herself dwelling on her memories. It was as if she had to remind herself of her own past to give herself the courage to fight for her future. Thinking about the present, about how her family would be feeling and how they'd be coping with her disappearance, that was too painful to bear. So she stuck firmly to the past. Now she was remembering a playground game she'd loved when she was little.

'What's the time, Mister Wolf?' was the teasing cry, uttered in mocking, singsong tones by the crowd of children. Adda-Leigh was one of the crowd. A boy with ginger hair, whose name she'd since forgotten, had been picked to be the wolf. He stood with his back to the others, patiently enduring their taunts.

'One o'clock,' he called out.

'What's the time, Mister Wolf?'

'Three o'clock.' Adda-Leigh advanced, step by step, closing in on the wolf, giddy with excitement, sick with anticipation.

But then came a different reply, uttered in a gruff roar by the wolf, who suddenly turned and rushed at the crowd, trying his best to seize the nearest squealing child. And Adda-Leigh ran, swift as a gazelle.

'Dinner time!'

That was the moment Adda-Leigh was waiting for now. Her stomach churned, but not with hunger. Her mouth was dry as dust and she felt an intense pressure on the back of her neck, as if in anticipation of a mortal blow. This, she knew, was fear. She was becoming all too familiar with the sensation.

At last she heard the footstep on the stair. He was bringing the tray of food. Dinner time. She stood up and got into position, flattened against the wall alongside the door.

It seemed to take an age for him to reach the passageway. Adda-Leigh listened, her heartbeat pounding through her head, as he walked up to the door, knelt down and pushed open the grill. Then there was silence.

Some fifteen minutes earlier, Adda-Leigh had rolled up her mattress, stretched her pullover over it and shoved it up against the grill in the foot of the door. Whether or not he really believed she was lying there, unconscious, was not important. The vital factor was what happened next.

She heard him straighten and then came the rattle of a key in the lock. For the first time since she arrived, the cell door was pushed open.

COLD SILVER

Sam lowered his head. He looked at the ground. He felt a fiery knot of bile burning in his throat. He swallowed, painfully, with effort.

'Now,' said the man who insisted Sam call him Master. 'Again. Extend your right wing.'

They were in the field behind the cottage. Dusk was gathering, but Master Richard showed no signs of ending the training session.

Sam stretched out. The muscles in his shoulders and back ached. The pain in his wing was sharp and unrelenting as he held it outstretched, trembling with effort. He gritted his teeth.

'Don't clench your jaw!' The voice of the Master cut through the cooling, midge-filled air. 'Relax. Accept the pain. Breathe. Now extend your left wing and hold still! I SAID STILL!'

Master Richard thrust his face close to Sam's, his silver-blue eyes fixed in a lock-tight stare. The man's cold breath hung in the air, smelling faintly of cloves and disinfectant.

Sam, his wings extended to their utmost, shook with exertion.

'You're still moving! Don't you understand the meaning of still?' Master Richard's eyes were wide with fury. 'How dare you disobey me?' He paced back and forth, flattening the grass beneath the heels of his calf-length combat boots. 'Standing there, shaking like a leaf. You're pathetic!'

Anger swept through Sam and he felt the fire burning in his throat again. He could have simply walked away. He knew he wouldn't have tolerated such treatment from Father David. But then Father David would never have behaved that way. Sam sensed that this man who called himself 'Master' was expecting him to fail, to give up. He was being goaded, pushed towards a response, as if the Master were testing him, trying to gauge the quality of his spirit. He swallowed his anger. If Master Richard wanted stillness then that's what he'd give him. Sam took a deep breath and held his features still and relaxed. He breathed in through the nose and out through the mouth. He managed to blank out the intense discomfort of his outstretched wings.

Their trembling subsided. He stood utterly still. His breathing slowed, growing quieter and deeper.

The Master paced up and down, casting him the occasional contemptuous glance, his white hair swinging on his shoulders. Soon Sam realised that Master Richard wasn't looking directly at him, but was glancing slightly to one side or the other. Sam's stillness had become complete. His Master could no longer see him. He felt the fireball in his throat slip back into his chest and dissolve in a glow of triumph.

This art of complete stillness was the first of his special powers that Sam had learned to control. It came naturally to him. It had helped that Father David had a particular interest in the technique himself and so had proved an inspiring tutor. Sam was able to slow his metabolism to a point very close to utter stillness. Even the blood moving through his veins slowed to a temporary stop. In that state he became very hard to detect. This, coupled with a telepathic aura that seemed to come as a natural extension of the condition, rendered him virtually invisible as long as he remained immobile. Even the keenest minds were unable to detect him.

At last the Master grunted and glanced up at the darkening sky. 'Very well. We shall now return to the cottage.'

They set off across the field. All around them bats

described wild, linear patterns through the inky sky or swept low over the thistle heads, feasting on midges and grass moths.

'A lot of animals are scared of me, but not the bats,' Sam said. 'Horses are afraid. And sheep. And dogs.'

'Domestic creatures. Slaves.' Master Richard sniffed derisively.

'There was a dog . . . back in England . . .' Sam spoke hesitantly; his low rumbling voice was full of regret. 'I think I may have hurt it. Hurt its mind. I didn't mean to. I was just afraid. I like dogs.'

'Slavering, craven beasts. A dog can be taught to imitate nobility, but at heart it will always be an animal. But what of you, Sam? Are you human or are you a brute beast? Or are you something else altogether?'

'I'm just a boy,' Sam said, miserably.

'You're much more than that. Now please, don't let me have to remind you again. For the duration of our time together, I must ask you to call me Master. It is essential to your training programme that proper disciplines are observed. Father David, alas, was terribly lax on that front.'

'Father David! I still don't understand. Where has he gone?'

'"Where has he gone, *Master*."'

Sam nodded and repeated the word in an embarrassed mumble.

'He has returned to Luhngdou. Now that I am Master of the Companions he was delighted to renew his allegiance to the organisation. He has gone to the land of his ancestors, and yours, to take up his duties as a Companion priest once more.'

'Did he leave anything for me – Master? A note? A message?'

'You were expecting a fond farewell?'

'No, it's just . . .' Sam broke off. He remembered the sensation he'd had in the ruined house, just before Master Richard had appeared. The sensation that Father David had wanted to say something to him, urgently. Whatever message the little priest had wanted to pass on, it seemed he hadn't confided in the man with the long white hair. Sam was convinced the Master knew more than he was willing to say. He claimed that, like Father David, he was training the dragon-boy to protect himself in a world hostile to his newfound inhuman state. And yet Sam couldn't shake the suspicion that Master Richard was actually testing his weaknesses. Why, he couldn't tell.

And despite his denial, he realised he *had* expected some parting words from Father David. Sam and the small priest hadn't always got on. But the man had tried to help him come to terms with his condition, had urged him to learn to control his powers, had tried to give him some kind of order and stability in his life, and there were times when Sam had resented it. But for Father David to simply up and leave without a word after the two of them had lived side by side for months seemed totally out of character. Something was wrong.

Sam looked at the Master striding over the field. He tried to open his mind to the white-haired man's thought waves, to gain an instinctive impression of his intentions and motives. But Sam could learn nothing that way. Master Richard was a blank page. It was as if the man had no thoughts or feelings at all. Or as if he had learned to mask his true nature, both inside and out.

Master Richard turned his head and looked up at Sam, his silver-blue eyes betrayed not the slightest flicker of humanity.

CROSSING THE LINE

Georgette stood by the police cordon, outside the burnt-out warehouse. The blue and white plastic tape shifted fitfully in the breeze. She could see no signs of activity, but there was a police van parked in the road. She touched the flimsy tape with her fingertips. It was tempting to just lift the cordon and slip through, but she knew the police would not welcome her interference. She'd already been told to leave the investigation to the professionals. If she trespassed on the site, they said, she might contaminate the crime scene and compromise all their efforts to find Adda-Leigh, or the white-haired bogus detective they now suspected of kidnapping her. It seemed that anything she did might make things worse for her missing friend. Georgette looked down at the tape. The bold capitals spelt out the order: POLICE – DO NOT CROSS.

Scuffling footsteps were approaching, together with the pad of paws on pavement. She didn't turn. She knew who it would be.

'All right, George? I reckoned I'd find you here.' Aaron's voice contained its usual self-satisfied tone. He sidled up beside her. Jaws was panting hard, pulling at the lead, but he quietened when he recognised Georgette. He licked her hand. She stroked his head absently.

'Don't call me George,' she said to Aaron, coldly. 'I'm not a man.'

Aaron shrugged. 'Sausage roll?' he said. He proffered a half-eaten pastry filled with pinkish-grey meat, wrapped up in oily cellophane.

Georgette wrinkled her nose in disgust and turned her back on him.

'Please yourself. Here you go, Jaws!'

Jaws chomped and slobbered on the sausage roll. Aaron brushed a few of the crumbs off his sweatshirt.

'You not been home yet then?' Aaron tried. Georgette was still in her uniform. Her school bag was on her shoulder. She'd been up to the warehouse every day that week, straight from school. She didn't get home until half past five or six o'clock.

Aaron sighed. Georgette ignored him. 'Look,' he said. 'How was I to know that detective wasn't for real? And the cops'll catch him sooner or later, now I've told them about him.'

Georgette said nothing.

'Oh, come on!' Aaron spread his arms. 'I helped look for Adda-Leigh, didn't I? I found that diary, didn't I?'

'Jaws found the diary,' said Georgette. 'And you're an idiot! You gave the kidnappers the information they wanted, whoever they are! Adda-Leigh might never have been taken if it hadn't been for you. You and your big, fat mouth!'

'Fat!' echoed Aaron, hurt. Georgette walked away from him, away from the warehouse. 'I'm on a diet,' she heard him say. 'Why d'you think I gave Jaws half that sausage roll?'

'Anything could've happened to her!' Georgette shouted as she hurried away, her footsteps ringing out on the broken pavement. 'She might be dead!'

Dead. The word seemed to echo around the empty factory buildings, hanging in the air like the vibrations of a tolling bell. Adda-Leigh might be dead. She'd said it at last, said it out loud. Georgette rushed on, desperate now to be home, her eyes blind with tears.

Georgette's dad was sitting at the table, newspapers spread out all around him, opened at the back pages, the classifieds, where jobs in catering and bar work were advertised. Unopened bills, their envelopes bearing the logos of a variety of credit cards, were piled on the floor beneath his chair. There was a red pen in his hand, poised above the newspaper. He looked up quickly when Georgette came into the room.

'Georgette . . .' he said, carefully. 'I wish you'd come home sooner. Puts the wind up me when I don't know where you are.'

'I told you where I was.'

'Is it a good idea, though love? It's not safe up there. Derelict old part of town, that is.'

'The police are there, looking for Adda-Leigh.'

'Yeah, well. I worry about you, that's all.' Georgette's dad ran a hand through his thinning hair.

She looked over his shoulder at the newspaper. A wobbly red circle had been drawn around an advert. *BARWORK — experienced staff wanted. Accommodation provided.*

'You said you were going to get some other kind of job, Dad. A nine-to-five job.' She looked at her father. He avoided her eye.

'I've tried,' he said. 'I got nowhere.'

'But you can't just go back to pulling pints. You were manager here!'

'It wasn't exactly a roaring success though, was it? Why d'you think we got closed down?'

Georgette slipped her school bag from her shoulder and let it fall to the ground. 'We'd have to move,' she said bleakly.

Her dad cleared his throat. He delved under the newspapers and brought out a letter written on green paper. Georgette recognised her mother's handwriting.

'She wants you to think about it.' He waved the letter, gently. 'You see, the thing is, when the advert says "accommodation provided" it means for me. But not for you. We wouldn't have the run of the place like we do here. What they're offering is just a room above some dodgy boozer. No place for a teenage girl to be living.'

'She wants me to think about what?' Georgette stared at the green paper, the familiar large looping scrawl, written in purple ink.

'They've got a big house, her and what's-his-face. Plenty of room. And she really does want you there.'

'York. You want me to move up to York? I was there at Easter. I know what it's like. You want me to live with Steve and his spoilt brat twins?'

'And your mother.'

'Yes. Her.' Georgette swallowed. She bit the inside of her mouth. 'You want me to leave London? Now? With my best friend missing, abducted, taken away?'

Her father cleared his throat again.

'Maybe it'll be for the best,' he said, staring blankly down at the piles of newspaper.

'How?' Georgette shouted. 'How can any of it be for the best, ever again?' She kicked her school bag across the floor. It subsided in a heap by the wall. Then she turned and stalked out of the room, a sick feeling rising from her stomach. Her eyes were stinging. But she was too numb for tears.

IN SHADOW

Father David peered into the corridor. At the opposite end, deep in shadow, there was a closed door. He took a breath and walked into the gloom.

At the door he stopped and listened. He could hear nothing but the gulls and the waves crashing, somewhere out beyond the walls. He grasped the door handle. Cold porcelain. The door opened without a sound.

It was another empty room. The same white walls, the same high windows. A door was set in the far wall. This door stood open, and led into a gloomy corridor. There was a movement, the swish of a flowing garment, a figure with long, black hair. A woman.

'Wait! Please!'

The small priest tried to dash across the room to

catch up with the mysterious woman but something was wrong. His knees buckled and he lurched forward, staggered, arms outstretched. His legs gave way and he tumbled to the floor. As he fell he saw, at the end of the corridor leading out of the room, another door, deep in shadow. The woman darted into the room and the door swung closed behind her.

CHEERFUL MESSAGES

It was easy. Too easy. The plan had been no plan at all. It was the sort of thing that happened in unconvincing action movies. The hero is a prisoner. He feigns illness and the guard investigates. The hero slips out the door, slamming it behind him – captor is made prisoner, prisoner is free! It was the sort of scenario Adda-Leigh would have scoffed at had she watched it on the screen or read it in a book. And yet it had worked. But as she hurried up the spiral stairs, her legs aching from the unaccustomed effort, it occurred to her that her captor hadn't actually made any effort to thwart her break-out. She had the uneasy feeling he knew something she didn't.

She climbed the stairs, gasping and panting, taking the steps two at a time. Her leg muscles screamed out for rest but fear pushed her on. The beam of her torch bounced ahead of her like a will-o-the-wisp, leading her onwards. There was no sound of pursuit.

The stairs coiled around a walled-in central shaft of unfinished concrete and each step was thick with dust. There was no tiling or ironwork or plaster facing, this way out had clearly never been in public use. The sound of the tube trains close by had led her to expect her prison to be in an obscure part of an Underground station. The spiral staircase reminded her of some older stations on the network, those that were accessed by lifts and stairs rather than by modern escalators. As she staggered on, the jolting beam of her torch illuminated a scrawled message on the wall: *KEEP GOING – JUST ANOTHER 84 STEPS TO GO!*

She smiled grimly. She imagined some jocular Underground maintenance man penning the message for the benefit of his fellow workers. So if this staircase was used by track repair teams then it should lead to a station entrance. She imagined a bustling ticket office. Lights. People. Ignoring the pain in her legs and the searing breath rattling in her chest, she continued to climb.

As she dragged herself on, she counted off the steps.

'. . . two, four, six, eight . . .'

Another cheerful message on the wall. *NEARLY THERE NOW, OLD SON!*

'. . . forty-eight, fifty, fifty-two . . .'

Wheezing and grunting with effort she forced herself up the last sweep of the staircase. She reached level ground, a passageway. She stumbled along it, her arms swinging, the torch pointed at the ground.

The ironwork shutter hit her like an oncoming train. Blindly, she'd slammed into it in the dark. The unexpected impact threw her backwards onto the bare, concrete floor.

She lay there, shattered and gasping, unable to grasp what had happened. The torch, still gripped in her hand, shone dully on the iron grill that barred the passageway. There was no way through.

On the wall there was another scrawled message. *HOPE YOU'VE GOT YOUR PASS KEY, MATE!*

EMPTY

Master Richard sat cross-legged on the bare wooden floorboards. In Sam's absence, the rooms of the cottage had been cleared with ruthless efficiency. The old armchair Father David had slept in was gone, as was all the other furniture. Now the rooms were bare, austere, cell-like and cheerless.

The Master's eyes were closed. His hands rested in his lap. He might have been asleep, except how could anybody sleep sitting so rigidly upright? Sam looked at him, the pale skin, the angular features, the long white hair falling to his shoulders. Although he was sitting in the classic meditation pose of a Buddhist monk, there was clearly no trace of any eastern element to his ancestry. The Master's forebears were probably Viking chieftains, Sam thought, and he imagined they would

fridge door with a yell of anguish, he swore furiously and kicked at the flagstone floor, his clawed feet sending sparks flying as they tore across the rough stone.

'You must learn to control your base emotions.' Master Richard was standing in the doorway, regarding Sam coldly. 'Is it any wonder you cannot harness your powers when the slightest thing sets you snivelling and whining like a baby?'

'I am *not* snivelling!' Sam curled his lip. A thin dribble of smoke curled from between his teeth.

'Boo-hoo-hoo!' the Master sneered. Sam shook with anger, but he said nothing. Once more, he sensed that the only way to cope with the Master was to play him at his own game. He decided to change the subject.

'So, Master,' he tried to make the word sound like an insult, 'where's the food?' His voice was a dark and furious bass rumble.

'That wasn't food. That was junk. It was poison. Tomorrow we will look into finding a more appropriate diet for you. As for tonight, we will eat nothing. Call it an exercise in self-denial.'

Master Richard turned on his heel and walked calmly out of the kitchen, leaving Sam staring at the ground, moodily belching out gouts of yellow smoke. He kicked at the floor again and thought about the absent priest. It struck him that he should put aside his resentment and try to make telepathic contact with Father David. He could ask him where he was, and whether Master Richard could be trusted or not. The priest didn't have a mobile phone, but there must be other ways to get through. Sam recalled the clear vision he'd had in the forest. He couldn't sense a presence anywhere close by, however. Perhaps Master Richard had been telling the truth and Father David had gone to Luhngdou, far enough away to make any telepathic contact impossible.

Frustrated, Sam shook his head violently from side to side, hunger pangs still gnawing at his innards. The head shaking had been a habit of his back before the changes had taken hold. The sharp pang of memory brought tears flooding into his eyes.

DINNERTIME

Georgette looked down at her plate. A pair of blackened sausages lay among a sprawl of soggy cabbage leaves and several dollops of mashed potato. A watery fried egg gazed up at her like a rheumy old eye. She pushed her chair back from the table.

Her father was buttering a slice of white bread, holding it in one hand and slapping at it with his knife. The slice flapped like a fish on a line.

'Aren't you going to eat?' He looked at Georgette, his forehead creased with concern and disappointment. 'You used to love this dinner.'

'Hmm,' Georgette said.

Events had moved on, rapidly. There had been more letters from York. Arrangements had been made. Georgette would be moving up north, to live with her mother. The fact hung between father and daughter like a curtain of silence.

'You know I had to accept that job.' Her father shifted in his seat. 'When this old place' — he gestured around him with his fork — 'is sold off, we'll be out on our ear. I had to do something. I can't stand by and see my own daughter put out on the streets, now can I?'

Georgette said nothing. The police investigation seemed to be going nowhere. There was less activity up at the burnt-out warehouse and nobody would tell her anything. The officers were polite, and sympathetic up to a point. But she could see in their eyes that they didn't really want to talk to her. She was becoming a nuisance. Well, it appeared they wouldn't have to put up with her for much longer.

She looked at her dinner. It was true, this used to be her favourite, back when she was ten, after Mum started working late, when Dad used to cook sausage and mash every night of the week. But now she couldn't eat a mouthful. In a few weeks she'd be hundreds of miles away, up in York, and nothing would ever be right again. She couldn't go. Not yet. It was suddenly clear to her. She couldn't go anywhere, she couldn't do anything, until she'd found Adda-Leigh.

A STEP AHEAD

A short, unlit corridor led from one empty room to another. Twelve paces across the bare floorboards there was another door, leading to another short unlit corridor, leading to another empty room. Father David paced from room to room. He found he couldn't maintain any sense of direction. He talked out loud as he padded from corridor to room to corridor again.

'Four identical rooms, arranged in a square, with a concealed entrance . . . somewhere. Am I right?'

There was no reply. No matter how he tried, he hadn't been able to catch more than a fleeting glimpse of the person he'd started to think of as his fellow prisoner. She was always in one of the other rooms, always a step ahead. When he slowed down, she slowed down. When he ran wildly from room to room, she outran him, closing the doors behind her to slow his pursuit. Was she afraid of him? Or was this some kind of bizarre game?

'Perhaps five rooms, arranged in a pentagon?'

Outside, the waves crashed and the gulls cried. Father David's footsteps beat out a plodding rhythm on the floorboards.

'It really is a most cleverly constructed prison.' He spoke calmly, but he knew his words would receive the same lack of response whether he shouted or whispered. He continued to speak, regardless, carefully suppressing his building sense of frustration. He had to get out. He had to find Sam and make sure all was well with the boy. 'The windows are too high and too small to even see out, let alone climb through.' Father David's voice remained level. 'And the entrance – there must be an entrance – is so well hidden it has completely defied all my attempts to find it. I suspect the way in and out is through a trapdoor in the flooring. Am I right? Am I warm or cold?'

Father David stopped in the doorway of the next room. Something was different. The room was utterly still. The gulls had ceased their shrieking and the sea itself seemed to be holding its breath. He took a cautious step forward.

'Hello? Is that –?'

The hairs stood up on the back of his head. There was something on the floor.

Father David swallowed. He stooped and picked it up. It was a small brass dragon, all sinuous coils and gaping jaws.

As he stood with the dragon cold and heavy in his hand, he felt numbness spread along his arm and through his chest and down into his legs. He opened his mouth to cry out but he could make no sound. All sensation left him in a blurry rush, as if a great wave had suddenly broken over him.

DESCEND IN DARKNESS

Adda-Leigh lay in the darkness of her own despair, somewhere deep underground.

'Come on, girl!' she whispered to herself. 'Get up! You have to keep it together!' But she couldn't force herself to so much as lift one hand. It seemed incredible that just a short while ago – a day? Two days? – she'd been on the point of regaining her freedom – or so she'd thought. Dully, she let the memory recycle itself once again.

Her disappointment at finding the passage at the top of the stairs closed off had been bitter indeed. Laid out on the floor, exhausted, her cheek pressed against the cold concrete of the top step, she'd listened, while her heartbeat slowed to something like its normal rate.

There was no sound of pursuit on the stairs. Her captor had left the keys in the cell door. She had slammed it shut and locked him in. He was, it seemed, trapped.

A quick sweep of her torch beam through the grill blocking the passageway was enough to tell her that her escape route had run into a dead end. The passage led to a fire door with a heavy padlock on the inside. There was no sound of human life beyond it. The busy ticket hall she had imagined so hopefully had been a desperate illusion. If she wanted to keep her chances of escape alive, she would have to retrace her steps, back down to her former cell, in which her captor was now incarcerated. She would have to follow the steps further down into the darkness and the unknown.

But when she reached the passage leading to the room where she'd been kept for so long, Adda-Leigh found she couldn't continue until she'd checked that the cell door was still secure. What if he'd got another key?

Creeping along the narrow, passage, her approach concealed by darkness, she reached out a hand and laid her palm gently against the surface of the door. The door shifted slightly. Something was wrong. She pushed. The cell door pitched and slid, scraping against the floor.

Adda-Leigh pressed her back against the wall and

switched on the torch. The door hung sagging in its frame. It had been ripped from its hinges. The cell beyond was empty. Her captor had escaped. And he hadn't needed a spare key.

Her breath deserted her. A moment of blind panic wiped her mind blank. To stand any chance of finding an alternative escape route, she would have to walk down the spiral staircase. And he was down there somewhere, in the dark, waiting. She flattened herself back against the wall and fought for breath.

It took Adda-Leigh a long time to subdue her sense of panic, and even longer to gather the courage needed to do what she knew she had to do. But at last she set out for the foot of the stairs. To stay where she was, outside the cell with the broken-down door, offered her neither security nor the chance of escape. The thought of remaining, doing nothing, simply waiting for her captor to return, was too terrible to contemplate.

'Adda-Leigh,' she said, whispering fiercely to herself in the darkness. 'You do not sit around and wait for trouble, girl. You go out and seize it by the scruff! Now, okay, you don't know what's down those stairs – but you're going to have to find out. It's time to make things happen!' She clenched her fists hard, but still she had to bite her lip to stop it trembling as she took the first steps down into the unknown.

She descended in darkness, keeping close to the wall, moving as slowly and as silently as she could. Her pounding heart seemed to echo around the curved walls of the shaft. She had the bizarre notion that she was somehow trapped inside her own chest and was walking down a spiral staircase into her own stomach. It occurred to her then, that she had been alone and imprisoned for far too long.

She reached the foot of the staircase without incident and switched on the torch for the briefest of moments. Ahead lay a short passageway. At the end of it was just blankness, a pitch-dark void. To her immediate left there was a doorway. She tried not to think who or what might be behind that door. She edged past and, with her back to the passage wall she felt her way along, step by step. Her groping hand probed ahead, palm flat against the rough cement of the wall.

Then suddenly there was no wall. The passageway ended in thin air. She stood still. A blast of air buffeted her face. A wind was springing up, gathering in strength. And then she heard it. A faint rattle, a hissing, a metallic singing, a low, guttural rumble. She knew then what the void was. She switched on the torch and saw the Underground tunnel, its sides decorated with dust-coated cables, and below them the gleam of the rail, through which many volts were passing, along which the tube trains hurtled. And from the clamour that now filled the tunnel she knew that a train would be passing any minute. A train full of people. People who might glance out of the window and see . . .

Adda-Leigh switched on the torch and held it below her chin, letting the beam illuminate her face. She was in a closed-down tube station. Or more likely a station that had never been opened, that had only been partially constructed, and then abandoned for some reason. It was used occasionally by track repair teams, she supposed, but obviously not very often. She was standing in an opening to a passageway that would have led to and from the platform. But no platform had been constructed.

Adda-Leigh began to wave her free hand, frantically, even before the headlamps became visible, lighting up the walls of the tunnel before the onrushing train. Then it came hurtling by, forcing a blast of warm air before it and almost knocking her off her feet. But she held the lit torch to her face and waved. And the train roared by carrying hundreds of people, barely a metre away. Light from the carriages danced over her, dazzling her with more illumination than she'd seen in she didn't know how many days.

But before the train had fully passed, a pale-skinned hand reached out from behind her and took hold of the torch, crushing the plastic casing in its merciless grip and extinguishing the feeble light for ever. Then the train was gone, and utter darkness returned.

Adda-Leigh screamed, high-pitched and prolonged. The scream was not simply born of fear. There was despair and disappointment, and anger too. Why had she been taken? What had she done to deserve this terrible treatment, locked away in darkness and silence? All she'd done was to go to meet someone who said he could give her some information about Sam's whereabouts. Someone who said they knew the truth.

In her terror and dismay she lashed out wildly with her fists, pounding at the torso of the man who stood behind her in the darkness. He made no attempt to shield himself from her blows. He didn't react to her assault at all. After a while her futile rage burned itself out and she stumbled, careless of where she trod. The ground seemed to vanish beneath her feet and she pitched backwards into the void, falling with a yelp of surprise, down towards the live electric rail in the tube tunnel.

How he had managed to catch her she didn't know. The darkness was so intense he surely couldn't have seen her. And yet, somehow, he snatched her up saving her from falling onto the track.

She was lifted back into the passage and laid gently on the floor. He brought bottled water, placed it in her hand, and she drank thirstily.

In a while, she spoke to him.

'Let me go. Please.'

'Soon,' he said.

'Why are you keeping me here? Let me go,' she said again, her voice dull with despair. He said nothing for a while, then his voice floated out of the darkness.

'Know this. I shall not harm thee.'

'What! But you *have* harmed me! Kidnapped me! Brought me down here! Locked me up in the dark!'

'What do you wish of me?' The voice sounded puzzled, as if the notion of another person's suffering was somehow extraordinary.

'Let me go.' Adda-Leigh turned her face to the passage wall. 'Just let me go.' After a while her captor moved away without another word and climbed back up the spiral stairs with a slow tread.

BREAKFAST ON THE LAWN

Master Richard stood in the sunlight that poured in through the cottage window. He held the small wooden rack in his hands. The rack contained a collection of sharply pointed skewers. The handles were of wood, brightly painted, the size of a hen's egg, and fashioned into a row of severe-looking heads, all slick with varnish.

Sam ducked under the door and shuffled over to look at the rack of skewers, intrigued.

'What's that, Master?' Sam's voice was still thick with sleep. The Master's training regime had left him exhausted. It was only the rumbling of his empty stomach that woke him up. That and Master Richard loudly chanting psalms outside his bedroom door. Sam was too tired even for anger.

The white-haired man held out the rack of skewers. 'These are the Wu Ying Chiang-Chun.'

He stared expectantly at Sam, who looked blank. Master Richard sighed.

'You have so much untapped potential. So many abilities you don't know how to use! Clearly linguistics is one of them.' He shook the rack and the skewers rattled against its bamboo sides. 'These are the Generals of the Five Directions. They are part of a Chinese temple-medium's equipment. They are spirits, invoked for protection.'

Sam leaned forward for a closer look. 'What do you do with them?'

'The medium takes them one at a time.' The Master took hold of the first head and withdrew the skewer, holding its steely point up to the light. 'He pierces his body with them. The first two through his cheeks, the second two through his arms or his calves. The last he thrusts into his tongue. Thus he summons the Five Generals, who each command a spirit battalion and protect the locality from attack.'

Sam winced. 'Does it work?'

Master Richard gave a chilly smile. 'The skewers are sharp enough to pierce the toughest hide.'

That wasn't what Sam had meant but he didn't pursue the question. In the silence, his stomach rumbled loudly.

'I'm starved!' he said. 'What are we doing about food, Master?'

Master Richard sighed again. 'Do you recall when your . . . special condition first became apparent to you? I'm sure you didn't eat for weeks!'

'Yeah, well.' Sam looked at the ground. 'That was different. I wasn't hungry back then. I am now.'

'Self-discipline!' Master Richard returned the spirit skewer to its place in the rack, which he stood on the window ledge. 'Has it occurred to you that you may not need to eat at all?'

Sam stared back blankly. Master Richard sighed again.

'However, there is a way to combine training with appetite,' he said, and he strode over to the front door, his long white hair swinging. Sam followed him out into the brilliant sunshine of the early summer's morning.

A post had been driven into the ground on the lawn in front of the cottage. A small white goat was tethered to the post. It looked up at Sam and bleated mournfully, lowering its head and backing away from him in alarm.

'What's this?' Sam said.

'It's your breakfast,' said the Master.

AN ANGEL AT HIS SHOULDER

Father David silently offered up a wordless prayer. He prayed for understanding. He could not make out what had happened to him but it was clear it had been triggered the moment he picked up the brass dragon. There was a stinging in his eyes and his hearing was muffled, as if his ears were covered by damp cloth, but still he had seen and heard everything.

The tethered goat, Sam stumbling away, spreading his wings and kicking at the ground, launching himself into the air, to glide across the field behind the cottage, his clawed toes barely clearing the thistle and the clover. All the while a man he couldn't see was laughing. Mocking laughter, which hung on the morning air.

'You are weak!' the man shouted after Sam. 'You must learn to be strong! Kill the goat! Eat your fill!'

Father David had seen Sam come to rest in an over-grown copse on the edge of the field. It seemed to the priest that he was floating just behind Sam, invisible, like an angel at his shoulder. He tried to speak, but found he had no voice. His thoughts raced in a wild and formless panic.

'How is this possible? How can I be seeing this? Is this a dream? A hallucination? God help me!'

Sam was clutching at his head. 'Stop it!' he bel-lowed. A stream of fire shot from one nostril and he writhed in pain, falling to his knees in a thick bramble patch.

Father David cleared his mind. Sam was obviously suffering, but what was causing him such agony? He felt a burst of deep concern for his charge. Here was the last of the dragon-folk of Luhngdou, his own kins-man, and he could do nothing to help him. Sam car-ried the ancient burden and blessing of transformation, carried it in his blood, without choice, without hope of a return to his old life. True, he was becoming a creature of great power with phys-ical and psychic abilities far beyond the reach of any human. And yet he was also a fourteen-year-old boy, a motherless child, miserable and alone, hiding in a belt of trees, far from anywhere he could truly call his home.

Father David knew it was impossible. He wasn't the

one with telepathic powers. This vision couldn't be real. It was an intense dream, brought on by the strain of his imprisonment and the damage to his memory.

And yet the vision was so convincing. He could see Sam, as if he was standing by his side. The priest's thoughts converged into a single impulse, a welling of sympathy. He let the boy's name ring through his head.

Sam.

Sam's head shot up and he looked around him, wildly.

'Father David!' he said. 'Where are you?'

It was only as the brass dragon slipped from his hand that the priest realised he was still clutching the ornament. He heard it clatter down onto wooden floorboards. The stinging sensation in his eyes faded away and he found himself staring up at the white-washed ceiling of his prison. His vision of the outside world, the belt of trees, Sam, had disappeared.

WAITING ON THE INSIDE

Georgette stood in the garden of the last house on Tow Road. The old electric fire and the mildewed mattress still lay discarded on the heap of rubble. The grass that Dandelion had grazed on was now tall and waving, as if the horse had never been there at all.

The house was empty. Georgette had checked every dank and derelict room. She was growing used to the silence of abandoned property, to the smell of decay and human waste that so often filled them, to the nervous churning of her stomach as she peered through broken windows or clambered in through battered-down doors, never knowing what or who she might find waiting on the inside.

It was dangerous and irresponsible behaviour, she knew that. She was putting herself at risk, and for what? The hopelessness of her search for Adda-Leigh was obvious now, even to her. She spent every evening searching the streets, coming home exhausted around eleven o'clock at night. She wouldn't speak to her father, never ate the dinners he left for her in the microwave. She rose late each morning and rushed from the house to avoid his worried gaze. At school she wasted the day away, just waiting for the search to begin again when the last bell rang at three thirty.

And since her argument with Aaron, she was on her own. Every evening, to her annoyance, she found herself actually missing his inane chat. And she missed Jaws too, panting and whining at his side.

But when Aaron had tracked her down at lunchtime, hiding behind a copy of *The Concise Oxford Dictionary* in the reference section of the school library, she had found it impossible to put aside her anger. He had told the bogus police detective about Adda-Leigh. And then she'd been kidnapped. It was all his fault.

'You're just beating yourself up, George,' he said. 'You ought to give yourself a break. Have a sherbet lemon.' He proffered the crumpled pack beneath the table, safe from the gaze of the librarian.

Georgette ignored him. She fixed her eyes on the book in front of her, which lay open at a random page.

'You looking up filthy words?' Aaron said, peering at the dictionary.

'No!' Georgette looked at him, her nostrils flaring angrily. 'It's a dictionary. There aren't any filthy words!'

'That one is,' he said, jabbing a stubby finger at the page. Georgette glanced down and then slammed the book shut, hurriedly.

'I wasn't even reading it!' she said. 'If you must know, I was trying to get some sleep.'

'Whatever you say, Georgie,' Aaron said, grinning.

Georgette shoved the dictionary hard and it slid across the smooth tabletop. The heavy book thudded into Aaron's chest and dropped into his lap. He let out a grunt of pained surprise. The pack of sherbet lemons hit the floor and the sweets scattered across the varnished floorboards like beetles running from the light. At her desk, the librarian looked up, frowning. But Georgette was already on her feet, walking out of the library.

And now, hours later, in the gathering dusk of the garden in Tow Road, Georgette wondered if Aaron had been right about her 'beating herself up'. Was that the reason she was spending more and more time alone and vulnerable in these abandoned places? Did she want something awful to happen? Surely not. What she wanted was to find her friend, Adda-Leigh. But the seeming impossibility of her search had left her desperate and close to hopelessness. And yet she would continue the search. She had no choice.

CONVERSATION IN DARKNESS

Adda-Leigh and her captor were talking. He was nearby, but it was too dark to see. She pressed her back against the wall, as she always did when she knew he was there. At least then she could be sure he wasn't behind her.

Her escape attempt hadn't made him angry. It hadn't prompted him to strengthen her prison or punish her in any way. Quite the reverse, in fact. He'd left the cell door broken and she was free to come and go as she pleased. The only thing he had done was to close off the passageway that led to the train tunnel with an iron shutter. He left her alone, most of the time, but occasionally, like now, she would hear his soft tread in the darkness and he would stand nearby, and seemed to want to talk. Their conversation tended to have one theme, however.

'Let me out of here,' Adda-Leigh said.

'Soon.'

'Why not now? Come on, you must! Just let me go!'

'You are not my enemy.'

'Then why do you keep me here?'

'You will bring him.'

'Who?'

'My enemy.'

'I won't. I promise!'

'You will! You must! I cannot release you. Do not ask it. What else would you have me do?'

Adda-Leigh thought for a moment.

'Fix the door to my cell. Put a bolt on the inside, so I can fasten it when I want to go to sleep. Let me have a light in there. Give me something to eat that isn't tinned soup. Give me a mobile phone so I can call my parents. And the police.'

There was a brief silence.

'You . . . fear me?'

'Of course I do! What do you expect?'

And now there was a longer pause before the soft and mournful voice spoke again.

'I can repair the door and give you the light. Those things shall be done.'

THE HAWAIIAN

The distinctive cardboard box lay on the tree stump, at the edge of the belt of trees. Five centimetres deep and thirty centimetres square, Sam would have known from the shape of the box what it contained, even without the printing on the lid: *BONITO'S PIZZA PASTA PARLOUR — Best Pizza to Go in County Cork!*

But he had no need to even see the pizza box to know it was there. The savoury aroma tickled at his nostrils, rich, unsubtle and, to Sam, utterly enticing. He looked out through the trees and saw it, gleaming white with red lettering, bright against the drab background of twisted vegetation.

Master Richard had left it there, on the far side of the copse. Sam could sense his presence, or more accurately the blankness that passed for presence, somewhere close by. But he couldn't see him. Control over his various senses was hard for Sam to maintain. He was still learning how to focus only on those sights, smells, sounds and sensations most useful to him at any given time. All the rest, birds in flight, insects boring into bark, a badger dozing in his underground set, and a hundred thousand other distractions, he tried to block out. As he peered through the trees at the pizza box on the stump he wondered if he was blocking out too much these days. He hadn't been aware of Master Richard's approach, and had no idea where he was hiding.

Perhaps it was because he was hungry, Sam thought. Or perhaps it was the shock of hearing Father David's voice out of nowhere calling his name, as clear as if the little priest had been standing at his side.

The priest had spoken once, then silence. Sam was left wondering whether it had been nothing more than a vivid piece of imagining, an audible hallucination. But the mysteries of his developing sixth sense were many, and he couldn't be sure what it was he had really heard.

A gentle breeze wafted the aroma of warm pizza towards him. How Master Richard had arranged for a take-away pizza to arrive miles from the nearest town, and for it to be still warm, Sam couldn't imagine. But that was of little concern to him now. He didn't stop to consider why the stern Master had changed his mind about feeding Sam fast food. Even the disturbing matter of Father David's disembodied voice would have to wait. Sam was going to eat pizza.

He pushed off the ground with a flick of his ankles, spread his wings and glided through the wood, skilfully banking and turning through the gaps between the trees. He scanned the area all around for signs of life. There was plenty of it, insects, birds and animals, but the only human for miles around was Master Richard, and even he didn't seem to be that close.

Sam landed by the tree stump. With one delicate claw he flipped back the lid of the box and lifted out a wobbling slice of pizza. He looked at the slice. It was edged with tendrils of melted mozzarella, and nestling among the cheese and tomato topping were chunks of pineapple and little pink squares of ham. It was a Hawaiian. Sam would have preferred a Four Cheese but he wasn't about to complain. He hadn't eaten for days. This, he told himself, was going to be good.

TO TAKE HOLD OF THE DRAGON

It took Father David some while before he could bring himself to take hold of the brass dragon once more. He had known of wonders all his life and he had seen many extraordinary things, not least the metamorphosis of Sam, from teenager to incipient dragon. But this was beyond his experience, beyond all his knowledge, and he was afraid. Picking up the little ornament had resulted in an instant vision of the cottage, of Sam fleeing in distress. Was it possible that this ordinary looking object, the sort of thing you might find for sale in a small cluttered shop somewhere on Tottenham Court Road, was actually a device for communication of the mind? Some kind of telepathic telephone? If it was, who had left it on the floor of his prison for him to find? There could only be one answer to that. His fellow prisoner, the woman in the white rooms.

His head ached and he longed to lie down on the bare floorboards and close his eyes. It was concern for Sam that galvanised him into action at last. Whatever it was he had seen, the vision had shown Sam in terrible distress. The little priest had dropped the brass dragon in his shock and it had fallen to the ground, breaking his connection with the vision. There could be no other explanation.

Now the dragon lay on its side, up against one of the bare white walls of Father David's prison. He sat down, close to it, his back leaning against the wall. Taking a deep breath, he reached out a hand and closed his fingers around the cold and heavy brass.

With his eyes stinging and his hearing muffled by a constant hissing, Father David found himself seemingly floating at Sam's shoulder once more. But this time he was ready to do what he could to help his charge. The boy was alone in a world that would never understand his developing dragon-state. Father David had been the only person able to guide him, to try to nurture his mental stability. The transformation could send those it afflicted insane, and a mad dragon-boy on the loose didn't bear thinking about. But now Father David had been imprisoned, by who, and for what purpose he couldn't yet tell. All he knew is that it left Sam in deadly peril.

Sam. The priest found him sitting in the sunshine, eating a pizza. At least, he had been eating a pizza. There was the box, the open lid smeared with globs of tomato sauce and dotted with grease spots. All the pizza had gone, except for one half-eaten slice lying discarded on the ground. A pair of bluebottles buzzed avidly around it. Sam himself was lying propped up against a tree stump with his eyes closed. He seemed to be sleeping off the effects of his recent meal.

Father David tried calling out to Sam but he couldn't seem to open his mouth. He didn't have a mouth. He didn't have any kind of body at all. Whatever it was of him that was actually there, looking down at Sam, was invisible and had no substance to it.

A shadow fell. A tall figure was standing there, dark against the sun. Father David recognised the man at once. Richard Smith. A bolt of alarm shot through the little priest. Something about this man, something urgent that somehow he couldn't quite recall. Was he held prisoner by the Companions, seized and incarcerated for desertion by command of their Chief of Operations? Father David called out a warning, not with his physical voice, but with his mind.

'Sam! Sam, wake up!'

Sam didn't stir. Father David watched the white-haired Companion walk over to where Sam lay and stand looking down at him. He suddenly drew back his booted foot and kicked Sam hard on the leg.

Sam shifted and groaned. A string of liquid flame trickled from the side of his mouth and fell hissing and crackling into the dry grass. The Master swung his right arm and cuffed the boy-dragon around the ear. Sam's head slammed back against the tree stump. His mouth fell open, revealing the double layer of needle-sharp teeth but he made no move to protect himself.

'You're weak!' said the Master. 'Weak, weak, weak! You can't lift a finger, but I know you can hear me. The drug I used on your disgusting food was an ancient blend of paralysing herbs I found noted in the journal of Vitas Jorgoon, the master dragon hunter himself. Your pathetic weakness has left you utterly powerless.' He aimed another savage kick at Sam's prone form.

Father David launched himself at the Master, in a desperate effort to force him back. The Master looked up, puzzled for a moment. He flapped at the air around his face, as if a fly were bothering him. That was all. He shook his long white hair and looked at Sam again.

'I'm sending you on a journey, Sam. Our time together has been most instructing. Now we must both move on, towards our destiny.'

Sam groaned again, his eyelids flickered and he

tried to lift his arm. His clawed fingers flexed, desperately, but then trembled into stillness. A puff of smoke rose from his nostrils and dispersed in the gentle breeze. Master Richard laughed harshly.

'You see, Sam, I know rather more about you than you thought I did. I know all your pathetic weaknesses, don't I? The priest you thought was your friend but who abandoned you. Adda-Leigh, the girl who'll never look at you again. Your father who doesn't love you, and your mother who left you when you were so young. I know all about them.'

Master Richard threw back his head and laughed. He strutted back and forth in front of Sam, braying a wordless victory chant to the trees and the dappled sunlight.

A group of men came out of the woods, carrying bales of thick rope and hefty scaffolding poles. They bound Sam, roped him to the metal poles and covered him with a length of plastic sheeting. They carried him off towards the track on the far side of the wood. Father David, helpless and invisible, watched until he could bear it no more, then he willed the brass dragon to slip out of his hand again.

CALLS AND MESSAGES

The phone was ringing. Georgette lay in the half-light of the early dawn with her eyes wide open. She woke early these days, around four o'clock, and rarely managed to get back to sleep. She would lie there, staring at the cciling, as the minutes turned to hours, until long after her alarm had sounded. But now the phone was ringing and she had to get up. She threw back her quilt and hurried out of her room to answer it.

'Hello?' She pressed the phone to her ear, fearful of what she might hear. There was something distinctly unsettling about a phone ringing in the early hours of the morning.

'George?'

She let out a hiss of breath through her nostrils

when she heard the uncertain voice on the end of the line. It was Aaron.

'What?'

'Sorry to wake you up and all that.'

'You didn't. What do you want?'

Georgette heard her father calling from his bedroom, his voice heavy with sleep. 'Who is it? What's happened?'

'It's nothing, Dad. Just Aaron. Go back to sleep.'

'Aaron? What's the matter with that kid! It's half past four in the morning, for God's sake!'

She heard Aaron cough nervously. 'Was that your dad?'

'Yes. Now what do you want?'

'I had to call you, George.'

Georgette waited for Aaron to go on.

'Listen – I'm scared.'

'I don't believe it! If you need someone to sing you a lullaby and tuck you up in bed because you've had a nightmare why on earth don't you wake your mum up instead of phoning me!' Georgette stopped to take a breath.

'No, listen, please! Someone rang my mobile. Just now, in the middle of the night.'

'Oh, for goodness' sake! It was probably just a wrong number!'

'I was asleep and my mobile went off. I grabbed it

and there was just this noise. Like the wind. Or like the sea. And I could hear a voice, right in the distance, shouting, screaming almost, but too far away for me to hear the words. It was horrible! Then everything cut out and there was nothing on my phone screen except this funny looking logo. Then that vanished too. It gave me a right turn. I had to call someone.'

Georgette had stopped listening. Her breath came in short and painful gulps. She remembered something Adda-Leigh had told her, months ago. How she thought Sam had been trying to get in touch with her on her mobile phone, and how a mysterious logo had appeared on the display screen.

Aaron was talking again. 'And the really weird thing is, that voice in the distance, I dunno why, but I think it might have been Sam!'

'The logo that came up on your phone,' Georgette said, 'was it a dragon?'

'Yeah. It was. How did you —' here was a tremor in Aaron's voice.

'You don't want to know,' Georgette said abruptly, and she hung up.

AGE

She sat with her back to the door. There was a light bulb fitted in the ceiling of her cell, with a cord switch. Now Adda-Leigh had light whenever she wanted it. There was a bolt on the inside of the door, just as she'd asked. She kept it fastened.

He was outside the door, she could tell. Though she had not heard him approach, some subtle sense told her he was there.

'Hello,' she said.

After a brief pause he spoke.

'Hello.'

There was a silence. Adda-Leigh was tired of silence. She had always been a talker.

'When are you going to let me out then? Today? Tomorrow?'

She was tired of being afraid. She babbled on, filling the void. 'Or are you waiting for me to get rescued by a knight in shining armour? I'm stuck here like some gormless princess in a tower.'

'Yes,' he said. 'I am waiting. I told you. But,' he paused then, uncertain, 'I am the knight.'

'What? No, no, you've got it all muddled up, boy! The knight is the one that rescues the princess. You must be the witch.' She giggled nervously at the thought, careless, now, of how he might react. 'I've never seen you properly, so for all I know you might be wearing a long black dress and carrying a broomstick over your shoulder.'

'I am not the witch. But you are Rapunzel. I heard the story, once, long ago. You are in the tower. The knight comes to your rescue. Your hair. He climbs.'

'It was a prince, I think,' Adda Leigh said quietly. 'Not a knight.' She was suddenly afraid again, and wished she hadn't been so talkative. The bolted door between them had made her bold, but she hadn't forgotten how he'd ripped this same door off its hinges when he'd been locked in the cell.

The impulse to speak out had not quite died away, however. There was something in her captor's voice that she had never noted before. A hesitancy, an unexpected youthfulness that spun her thoughts around. Who was he? What was he?

'What's your name?' she said. 'How old are you?'

There was a long pause before her captor answered. Adda-Leigh waited, wondering fearfully how he might react to such direct questioning.

'Call me Ishmael,' he answered her at last. 'I am fourteen years old.'

THE NAMING

BOSNIA-HERZEGOVINA – 1993

Father David turned to leave. The farmer called out to
him. The young priest caught the drift of what he was
saying, although he didn't know the language well.

'What's he want?' said Mrs Hare.

'He's asking what he should call the child. He wants
me to give him a name.'

The boy clung to the farmer's hard-faced wife. She
looked at him with puckered brows, her face drawn.
The priest couldn't read her expression. The child
glared sullenly up into the woman's lined and weath-
ered visage.

'Surely they can think of a name themselves,' said
Mrs Hare.

Father David cleared his throat.

'Ishmael,' he said. 'They should call him that.'

'Ishmael?' Mrs Hare raised her eyebrows.

'From the Book of Genesis.' Father David turned away. Mrs Hare followed him to the door. '"His hand will be against every man, and every man's hand against him."'

'Oh, Father, that's not very nice!'

The priest shivered. 'Perhaps I'll feel better when we've left the war zone,' he said.

BOXES WITHIN BOXES

'Father David?' Sam's voice was low and the words slurred, spoken with a tongue a little too large for easy speech, through two rows of sharp teeth.

'I am here.'

'Just checking,' Sam rumbled. His voice echoed around the sheet metal walls of the container. 'One minute you're there and the next you're not. And since I can't see you . . . whatever you are . . .' Sam trailed off.

'You still think that I am a hallucination?'

'Are you telling me you're not?'

'I thought I was the one who was dreaming. Now, all I know is that we are in a situation that, although extraordinary, seems to be reality. You have been imprisoned in a wooden box, now destroyed, inside a metal container, aboard what seems to

be a ship or boat. I am a prisoner at an unknown location, but I am able, through making contact with a small brass dragon given to me by an elusive fellow prisoner, to see and hear all that you are doing and, indeed, to converse with you as if I were nothing more than a voice in your head.'

'And this is reality?' Sam said doubtfully.

'Apparently so. And under the circumstances our only course of action is to assume so and behave accordingly.'

Sam shrugged. 'Okay. Let's go with the flow.' He gazed dully at the heap of charred and broken planks, the remains of the crate he'd been nailed up in. 'It's good to have someone else around, even if you are just a –'

'Please. I thought we agreed . . . !'

'Okay! Okay!' Sam winced. His head hurt, and the priest's voice wasn't helping, raised in protest, somewhere inside his mind. With one clawed toe, he poked at a piece of splintered wood. He felt a spasm of nausea as he recalled his time in the wooden crate, the panic he had felt on regaining consciousness and finding he was boxed up.

And the sickness had been terrible, a reaction to Master Richard's drug-laced pizza, made worse by the heaving of the Irish Sea. Sam had vomited great gouts of sodden ash. Not pleasant, in a confined space. He had howled. A terror had gripped him, a claustrophobic panic, and he had lost all control, destroying the crate and bringing down excruciating agony on his already exhausted and pain-wracked body.

The voice of Father David had spoken to him, calmed him, helped him to counter the effects of the nausea and pain through slowing his breathing and lying still, among the ruins of the crate.

He had escaped one box only to find himself in another. Through the metal walls of the container, came the unmistakable sounds and smells of a vessel at sea. Fumes hung in the air and the ship's engines thrummed, sending a constant vibration up through the deck.

'Sam. We need to try to understand the forces that are ranged against us, to deduce what their motives might be. Richard Smith, the Master of the Companions, has arranged your capture, and doubtless is also behind my own imprisonment —'

'Please, can't it wait? I'm feeling awful!'

A great shiver ran through Sam. Another wave of nausea passed over him. He retched. Dark smoke filled the container.

'You're not going to be sick again are you?' Father David sounded worried.

Sam shook his head slowly. A terrible anxiety at the dim memory of something Master Richard had said broke over him again. Just before Sam had fallen into deep unconsciousness, the Master had mentioned

Adda-Leigh. What did he know of her? Was she in danger, because of her connection with Sam? If so, any harm she came to would be his fault.

Sam's first reaction had been to reach out with his mind and find her. He knew he could do it, but he hadn't properly mastered the ability to seek someone out, to communicate telepathically, directly from mind to mind. That hadn't stopped him trying.

His wild efforts had fallen short of their mark. For a few terrifying moments, all the ship's crew were assailed by phantom voices and sudden numbing attacks of anxiety caused by Sam's telepathic stumbling. The boat nearly foundered in the rough sea as those on board struggled to retain their sanity.

Again, Father David had intervened.

'The crew of this vessel are no doubt in the pay of Master Richard. But if the ship sinks it will benefit no one.'

The priest had persuaded Sam to concentrate on something he knew he could do – send a message to a mobile phone. He had tried Adda-Leigh's number at first. He failed to make any kind of contact. Then, at Father David's suggestion, he had switched his attention to Aaron, whose number he also knew by heart. Sam had hoped to speak to Aaron, longed to hear his old school friend tell him that Adda-Leigh was perfectly safe, at home with her family, going about her ordinary human life. But his physical and mental condition had not been up to the task. Although he'd made contact, Aaron hadn't been able to understand anything he'd said. He'd quickly lost the signal and had been unable to find it again. Now he was too exhausted to do anything except lie stretched out on the floor of the container and worry.

But the voice of Father David filled his head once more.

'I am convinced Master Richard is your mortal enemy, Sam, you need to know ...'

'Later,' Sam said. He groaned and clutched at his stomach.

Father David fell silent.

CHASING GHOSTS

Georgette knew the name of the detective sergeant in charge of investigating Adda-Leigh's disappearance. She knew the names of the detective constables on his team. She'd spoken to them all after she and Aaron had found the diary, and many times since. But none of them would see her now. Only WPC Johns, the police-woman who liked Bovril, was available to update her on the progress of the investigation.

'You'll just have to let them get on with their job, luvvie.' She flicked the switch on the electric kettle and sorted out a couple of mugs. 'I know you're her best friend and all, but we've got her mum and dad to look after, too, you know.'

Georgette blinked. She hadn't been able to face Adda-Leigh's parents, their terrible, endless anxiety was too much for her to bear.

'When we know anything we'll tell you straight away, I promise. In the meantime, have you considered counselling? It's very traumatic, what you're going through. There'd be no shame in asking for professional help.'

Georgette said nothing. She reached into her school bag and pulled out a folded newspaper. *The Marshside Free Advertiser* had been pushed through the door of the old Ferryman's Arms that morning. She quickly leafed through several pages filled with reports on disputes over refuse collection, antisocial neighbours and a knifepoint robbery in the local park. When she'd found the page she was looking for, she passed the paper over to the policewoman and sat back.

'What's this? "Local man goes for baked bean record"?'

'Not that story. The other one.'

' "Ghost Train! Commuters haunted by apparitions on the Underground"?'

'Read it.'

The policewoman shook out the newspaper to straighten the page. She scanned the article.

'Could you pass it on to the detective sergeant?' Georgette said. 'Please.'

Constable Johns lowered the paper and looked at Georgette.

'This is a story about some people on an Underground train who think they saw a ghost in the tunnel.'

'They saw the face of a young woman.'

'Well one of them said it was a young woman.' The policewoman folded the newspaper. 'Someone else said it was a creepy looking bald bloke. But I'll bet you most of the people on that train didn't see anything at all.'

'That doesn't mean there was nothing there! And they heard screaming!'

'Yes. Ghostly screaming, apparently.' Constable Johns threw the folded paper down on her desk. 'You want me to tell the DS to go chasing after ghosts?'

Georgette looked at the floor. 'It might be her. It might be Adda-Leigh.'

The policewoman puckered her brows and looked at Georgette.

'You know, love, I wish you'd go see a counsellor. I'm worried about you, truly I am.'

Georgette said nothing. She heard Johns sigh and pick up the newspaper. 'I'll make sure I pass this on. Now you need to get to school. I'll sort out a squad car to drop you round.'

HANDS

Fourteen. He was fourteen. Adda-Leigh paced around her dusty cell, with the door firmly bolted on the inside. Her mind was whirling. What sort of fourteen-year-old can rip a door off its hinges? What sort of fourteen-year-old kidnaps another teenager and holds her captive in an underground cell? And then tells her fairy stories?

And where was he now? Down in his storeroom by the track, where he kept the tins of soup he fed her on? Or was he outside the door to her cell again? He seemed to have the ability to move through total darkness, if he chose to, without making the slightest sound. When she heard his step, she now realised, it was because he wanted her to.

The more she discovered about her captor the more

confused she became. Was she less afraid of him, now she knew he was her own age? Or did she fear him even more? She had never even seen his face. Just his pale hands as he passed her a tray of food, or as he pulled the torch out of her hands down by the track.

The fetid wind blew up the stairs and into her cell and a tube train rattled by. Adda-Leigh had grown so used to the sound that now she barely registered it at all. But as the noise of the train died away a less familiar sound became apparent. She had never known Ishmael to climb the spiral stairs to the blocked passageway up near the surface. But he must have done so, because now she heard footsteps descending. He was making no effort to remain silent today. In fact, he seemed louder than usual.

Adda-Leigh tipped her head to one side and listened. A sudden fear of the unknown gripped her. It wasn't just Ishmael coming down the concrete stairs. She could hear two sets of footsteps. There was somebody with him.

UNCONTAINED

'*Are you fully rested, Sam?*'

'I'm okay, yeah.'

'*You will need to be closer to London if you're going to find Adda-Leigh. With your telepathic skills as untrained as they are . . .*'

'Yes, yes, I know! I should have listened to you and worked harder.'

'*Quite. The time has come to take our leave of this place.*'

'We have to find her. I have to know she's okay.'

'*There's nothing to say she is in any danger.*'

'That madman mentioned her, didn't he?'

'*Surely we would do better to concentrate on Richard, to discover his plan, his motives, his whereabouts?*'

'He's here. He's on the boat.' Sam's tone was grim. 'I can sense him. He's like a blank space, but I've learnt to recognise him now. Somehow he's able to block out his thoughts, his feelings.'

'Of course. He studied meditation and mind-clearance techniques at the Companion's seminary on Luhngdou. I remember hearing he was a particularly gifted student. So, let us discuss the so-called Master . . .'

Sam shook his head wildly from side to side.

'No! I have to be sure he hasn't got to Adda-Leigh! What else can I do? I can't just forget about her. Ever since we came to Ireland I . . .' Sam broke off and looked down.

'Yes,' said the voice of Father David. *'Of course. I cannot read minds, Sam, but I was aware of your suffering. The drawings in the sand . . .'*

'You saw the drawings?' Sam felt the hot rush of embarrassment.

Father David changed the subject. *'This sea crossing is a lengthy one. In truth, it would probably be safer to wait until the ship has docked and the coast is clear before we disembark. But, given your feelings, speed would seem to be of the essence and you will be far quicker travelling under your own steam. If you can leave this vessel now, I expect you'll be able to reach London before Master Richard.'*

'Leave? How?'

'You are stronger than you think, Sam. Use the anxiety you are feeling, the discomfort. Harness the anger you have

harboured against the Master. But remember, Sam, be careful not to go too far.'

'What do you mean?'

The voice of Father David was grave. *'You are quite capable of sinking this boat and killing everyone aboard it.'*

MENTAL

'Well, of course, they didn't believe me!' Georgette glared at Aaron. It was lunchtime. He'd found her in the corridor on the Languages Block, staring out the window. 'That policewoman thinks I've gone mental, waving crackpot newspaper stories about ghosts under her nose!'

'But you said you thought that was Adda-Leigh, not a ghost at all! You were well pleased when I gave you that newspaper!'

'But the police aren't going to take it seriously, are they? I wouldn't if I was them!'

Georgette's nostrils flared. She clenched her fists and let the anger burn through her.

'Well, it's not my fault,' Aaron said.

Georgette punched him on the arm.

'Ow! What was that for?'

'An early birthday present.' Georgette stalked off along the corridor. She left Aaron rubbing his arm. He called out after her. 'That policewoman was right. You have gone mental!'

Georgette spun round and glared at him.

'We have to search the Underground. Not just the local tube station, I've already looked there. That newspaper story is the only lead we've got. And Sam's been trying to contact you. There has to be a connection. Something's going to happen. I just know it.'

'But we can't go looking on the track!' Aaron threw up his hands. 'We'll be squashed flat by a tube train, or fried by the electric current on the line, or arrested by the Transport Police!'

Georgette shrugged. Aaron slapped his hands to his forehead.

'George! You're totally insane!'

'So you keep saying.'

She turned her back on him and walked away.

PHYSICAL

Sam raised his right leg. He spread his clawed toes and aimed his heel at the metal door of the container. There was great strength in him. He realised that his powers, both physical and mental, had been building up since he first came to Ireland and that he had no real idea what he was capable of. His muscles were poised and ready. He let himself remember the humiliations Master Richard had tried to inflict upon him. Fire burned in his throat at the memory. Then he cleared his mind and let his physical side take over, the part that remained in tune with his sinews, his bones, his teeth and his claws. It was as if his body had told his mind to sit back and enjoy the ride. His right leg shot out and his foot slammed into the door with a mighty clang. He followed up with a blow from his palm. He battered and tore and worried at the lock, hammering at the metal container without stint. The noise created was like the manic tolling of a giant, cracked bell. The door capitulated swiftly. Sam burst out and leapt down onto the deck.

His eyes adjusted to the sunlight in an instant. He was on the after-deck of a trawler. The nets and buoys had been cleared away and the mast had been fitted with pulleys and ropes by which the crew had, presumably, winched the metal container aboard. They'd kept Sam imprisoned where this converted fishing boat had once emptied its nets of helpless, flapping fish. But Sam was no fish out of water. He was at home in any element.

A ring of half a dozen men stood waiting for him, dressed in oil-stained overalls and donkey jackets. They all held weapons of some kind, a wrench, a club, a heavy iron spanner. Sam's gaze passed over them and their faces blanched with horror as they stared at what had emerged from inside the container. They stood frozen, slack-jawed with shock and terror, their weapons forgotten in their hands. Clearly the sight of Sam awake and angry was more than they could stand.

And Sam's physical side was still in control. These men were just another door to be broken down. Father David's voice was calling out a warning, but he couldn't distinguish the words. He ignored the voice, and felt the flames boiling up in his throat. His jaws parted and he screamed with pain and fury. The men on the deck scattered, yelling and gibbering in their panic.

Sam saw the men running and yanked back his head. Flames shot from his mouth and his scream filled the wind-whipped air. A fireball arched over the fleeing crewmen and engulfed the wheelhouse. Sam crouched then sprang. Pushing against the deck, he hurled himself into the air. He kept his wings folded and used the force of his leg muscles alone to propel himself, somersaulting over the grimy, orange-painted funnel. His foot clipped the rotating navigation radar and sheared it in two and he landed with a heavy thud on the blazing roof of the wheelhouse. He ignored the flames; they couldn't penetrate his fireproof hide. Somewhere deep inside he remembered that he was angry, and that the focus of that anger was here somewhere. He paused for a second, crouching amid the flames.

'Sam! The fire! Put it out!'

Father David's urgent shout came into focus but Sam ignored it. He knew that Master Richard was still in the wheelhouse. Grasping the edge of the roof with his clawed fingers, Sam swung himself forward, drawing his knees up into his chest as he rolled in the air and smashed through the wheelhouse window in a shower of broken glass. The small of his back slammed against the ship's wheel, buckling it out of shape. The boat slewed violently to port. Sam stood up and shook himself like a dog emerging from a swim in a lake. Pieces of glass dislodged from his scales and tinkled to the deck like hard rain. But Master Richard was nowhere to be seen. He had fled the wheelhouse and disappeared below decks.

'Sam! Please! Leave this boat, now! The damage you have wrought will slow them down considerably. We will reach London long before they do. Now, please, I beg you, leave these men to save themselves and be gone!'

'But they are my ENEMIES!' Sam roared out the word.

'Sam. Show mercy.' Father David's voice was calm and quiet.

Wings pumping at the sea air, Sam sprang back out through the gaping window and down onto the metal railings at the bows. The rails sagged beneath his weight. He swung his head and gazed around the deck. There was no one to be seen. Every living soul aboard the boat was hiding from him, gripped by terror and disbelief. He had even put Master Richard to flight.

But Sam could have killed them all. The sudden realisation filled him with horror and disgust. The truth of Father David's warning hit him. He felt less than human. A new rage, born of despair, burned through him, and he kicked off from the ship's side, causing the trawler to roll and dip beneath the force of the blow. He flew straight up into the boiling grey clouds, his wings whipping at the air. He turned, three hundred feet up, tucked back his wings and fell like a meteor screaming to earth.

As he burst from the clouds he let out another great plume of fire. The flames hit the water alongside the boat, throwing up a cloud of steam through which Sam dived, a split-second later. Down he plunged, and the sea swallowed him in an instant.

III

Firestorm

THE MONSTER AND THE WORM

Deep in the cold water, Sam moved as fast as any killer whale. Streamlined by instinct, with his limbs held close to his body, his feet pumped the water, powering him onward. He could sense the mainland, the Welsh coast up ahead, through miles of dark water. A pod of dolphins scattered as he passed, clicking out a chitter of alarm calls.

All that had happened to him over the past months spun through his mind. The loneliness, all his lovelorn moping and the mind-numbing boredom of his indolent days before Master Richard arrived, then the sense of betrayal and bewilderment as events had taken a more sinister turn. His current situation was that of anxious confusion, with Adda-Leigh in danger, Father David a disembodied voice and himself a creature of wild, thoughtless action, barely able to control the potentially deadly powers he possessed.

All he knew was the need to get back to London as quickly as possible. He neither knew nor, at that moment, really cared if it was the right thing to be doing. For the first time, he was allowing his altered body complete freedom. The violence of his escape from the container had released something in him. Now, out over the sea where he knew he could do nobody harm, he didn't even try to rein it in.

He headed for the surface and burst into the sunlight in a shower of spray. He opened his wings and dragged his dripping body into the air. A flock of gulls flew from him, shrieking. He knew he was close to land.

Streaking low over the surface of the water, the downdraught of his wing-beats churning the waves, Sam spat a dart of flames before him and then instantly overtook it. The fire sizzled into the sea far behind.

'Fly! Scatter! Run away!' he bellowed into the wind and the flying spray, his voice a harsh roar across the desolate surface of the sea. 'It's me, Sam Lim-Evans! I'm a monster! A MONSTER!'

He landed on a wooded hillside and crawled on his belly through the undergrowth, snaking his way uphill. He could hear the loud bleating of sheep from the fields beyond the wood. Their harsh, desperate cries broke out intermittently, grating and unsettling. Sam scrambled through the wood, too exhausted now to fly or even walk upright.

He crested the hill and reached the edge of the tree line. The wind hit him, as if it had lain in wait and then pounced. There was a grey-walled farmhouse with small blank windows. It stood in a field of thin grass that bowed down, abject beneath the unceasing wind. Sam turned from the sight of human habitation and headed back into the wood. He had to rest, he knew that, and he decided to allow himself an hour.

As night fell he came upon the ruined watchtower. No more than a stump of the tower remained, a circle of stones and mortar two metres high, surrounding half-a-dozen moss-covered steps, the remnants of a spiral staircase. All that was left of a medieval fortress, built, no doubt, by some English king intent upon dominating the Welsh. Sam's father had bored his son with lectures on the perfidious English. It had all seemed so distant to a London schoolboy in the twenty-first century. But now here he was, in this blood-soaked country, where his ancestors had fought and died to protect the rights of their ancient kingdom.

Sam crawled through the narrow doorway and pressed himself against the inside walls of the old tower. Were they still his ancestors, the Welsh, now that he had changed so much? He recalled Grandma Evans telling him about the red dragon of Wales. But flags and banners were a long way from the horrifying physical reality he'd now become. What real kinship could he claim with his father's people, or even his mother's forebears, out in the South China Sea? The dragon-strain had been buried deep within his genes. Few Luhngdonese had had to suffer the transformation that had taken hold of him. He would be the last.

'I'm not Welsh and I'm not Luhngdonese,' he whispered to the dripping walls. 'I'm a worm. Just a worm.'

FLOWN

The helicopter flew low over the surface of the water, the downdraught of its blades adding to the disturbance of the waves. It approached the stricken trawler. On board the fire in the wheelhouse had been put out. But the hours of effort to repair the damage Sam had caused to the steering had proved ineffective.

Master Richard watched the helicopter approach through a pair of binoculars. He noted the emblem on the side of the craft, a purple semicircle with the straight edge vertical. The insignia of the Companions.

He raised his voice above the howl of the wind.

'Prepare to secure a line. I shall be hoisted aboard the helicopter. As to the rest of you, you have been paid well for your trouble. I shall see to it that you receive full compensation for the damage to the boat.

And remember, your continued silence will be total. On pain of death.'

The hired crewmen looked sullenly back at the Master but none of them doubted his ability to make good his threat.

Master Richard turned to windward and took off his cap. The sea breeze caught at his long silver hair. He smiled. He would be on land again within the hour. A phone call to London, to where the faithful Crisp was waiting for instructions, would ensure that Sam's escape would prove no more than a minor hitch.

WORM IN THE MIND

'I'm a worm,' Sam told himself once again. A voice in his head interrupted him.

'Self-pity, Sam. It's an annoying trait.'

'You still with me?'

'I've never left you, though you have chosen to ignore me.'

'Well don't hang around on my account. You might be better off trying to get out of that prison you're in. Build a tunnel or something. And don't bother lecturing me about self-control. That's all *he* used to go on about, my so-called Master!' Sam uttered the word with a grimace of disgust.

'You could have killed someone, Sam, out on the trawler.'

'I didn't though, did I? I just want to forget about it.' He turned his face to the wall.

Father David was silent for a while. Then Sam heard

the familiar voice again, speaking in his head.

'What are you going to do?' There was an uncertainty in the priest's voice that Sam hadn't noticed before.

'I'm going to London. When I get close enough, I'll be able to find Adda-Leigh. I'll see if I can get through to Aaron again too. I should be able to reach his mobile from here.' Sam sucked in a great gulp of smoky breath. 'If she's in any kind of danger, if they've hurt her at all, I'll –' Sam's rumbling speech choked into silence at the thought of what he'd do.

'What if she is perfectly fine?'

'Then great, I'll come and bust you out of prison and we'll go get the Master.'

'You realise Master Richard knows you will be heading for London. In fact, that's probably why he mentioned Adda-Leigh in the first place, so he could predict where you would go if you escaped.'

'Look, I just need to make sure she's okay.'

'Sam. We don't even know why Master Richard had you captured, why he's had me imprisoned, or who my fellow prisoner might be. Don't you think we should think about these things?'

'Not until I know Adda-Leigh is safe. Now let me rest!' Sam closed his eyes firmly.

Alone with his own anxious thoughts, Father David watched over the resting dragon-boy.

THE DRAGON DISAPPEARS

Georgette sat in front of the open textbook. A sheet of lined paper lay on the desk beside it. She had written the date in the top right hand corner. She had written her name in the top left and the title in the centre of the page, underlined twice in pencil. The rest of the sheet was blank. She glanced up at the clock on the wall. There was only fifteen minutes of the lesson to go. Six months earlier she had been considered an excellent student. High grades had been predicted. That was then. She was a different person now.

She leaned her face in her hands and gazed out of the window to watch the empty crisp packets blow across the tarmac by the new unit. Someone was there, lurking near the steps. When he caught sight of her looking out, he began to wave his arms frantically. It was Aaron.

He waved and beckoned, eyes wide, beseeching.

Georgette stood up and hurried to the door.

'Where are you off to?'

Mr Hay. She'd almost forgotten he was there. She turned. The class were all looking at her.

'Toilet, sir.'

'No you're not. You've done nothing but stare out of the window all lesson. You can wait for the bell. Now sit down.'

'Sorry, sir. I'm not feeling well.'

'Georgette!' Mr Hay's tone was stern but she didn't look back. She ran down the corridor and out through the entrance by the Humanities corridor.

Aaron was waiting for her outside.

'Quick! Over here!' he said, taking her arm and pulling her along, ducking behind the unit, out of sight from the main building. Georgette pushed his hand away.

'This isn't a game, Aaron. Now what do you want? And this had better be important!'

"'Course it's important! I'm supposed to be in PE. If old Slough catches me I'll be for it.' Aaron held up his mobile phone.

'The text . . .' Aaron's face was deathly serious. 'Read it.'

Georgette looked at the mobile. There was a text message displayed on its screen.

Is Ad-Le ok? Mst knw.

Beneath the message there was a logo. A Chinese dragon.

'I don't know what to do. Should I reply to it or what? Do you think it's from –?'

Georgette interrupted him. 'It's from Sam, of course it is! And yes, I think you should reply!'

'It's weird though. There's no phone number, just that little dragon thing.'

Georgette blinked. The dragon had disappeared.

'Hold on,' she said. 'Something's happening.'

The text began to flicker. One by one the letters disappeared and the entire message vanished before her eyes.

THE NEW WORLD

Ishmael sat with her in the back seat. To stop her calling out, she supposed. To stop her screaming. Not that anyone was around when they came out of the empty building at the back of West Street, next to the closed-down paper-plate factory. They'd picked their moment well.

Adda-Leigh had never really seen Ishmael before. Not in the light. Any thoughts of screaming for help dried in her throat as she looked at him. Too tall for the car, he sat hunched, his head jammed against the roof. He held a hand up to cover his face but she saw his eyes, blinking at her through the gaps between his fingers. Pale-grey eyes, almost silver.

Fourteen. Could this creature be fourteen years old? He was pale as moonlight, veins and sinews clearly visible beneath his translucent skin. Muscles knotted his arms and neck. Although she knew he was immensely strong, his every movement spoke of pain, constant pain. He was completely bald, and had no eyebrows or eyelashes. The skin was puckered and wrinkled around his eyes, and his cheeks sagged like a man of seventy. But there was a warped youthfulness about his pallid features. Adda-Leigh was inclined to believe what he had told her. He was only fourteen. What terrible things had happened to him, she wondered, to leave him looking like this? He was like no fourteen-year-old she had ever seen before.

Except, perhaps, for one. Something in the young man's eyes, locked in a ruined face, reminded Adda-Leigh of the last time she'd seen Sam. She had seen him, spoken to him, as he hovered outside her window on a pair of wings that stretched out from his scale-encrusted shoulders. Her world had changed that day, just as surely as Sam's had. Ishmael was a part of the new and frightening world she found herself in.

She couldn't scream. She couldn't call out. The driver turned and looked at her. Adda-Leigh was seized by a paralysing jolt of fear. She recognised the man behind the wheel. It was the man who'd murdered the old woman over on the marshes. The man who'd pointed a gun at Adda-Leigh, who'd wanted to kill her.

TEN THOUSAND METRES

Glimpsed through a break in the cloud; England, spread out like a map. Field and forest, towns and motorways, like a mosaic pattern, shaded in soft browns, greens and gold. A river snaked across the land, winking in the sunlight like a quicksilver serpent.

Sam's wings beat the air. His mind reached out, searching for any sense of Adda-Leigh's whereabouts. He'd already sent Aaron a text message, which had proved a lot easier to manage telepathically than an actual phone call. The trouble was, he realised, Aaron would have had no way of replying. And what would happen to the message when he switched his thoughts elsewhere? He realised he should wait until he'd tracked down Adda-Leigh before calling up any rein- forcements.

From the still distant streets of London, Sam had now begun to get some scraps of psychic feedback. He would have to be patient. If he absorbed the sensations, bit by bit, he could then build a detailed picture of where Adda-Leigh was. He was improvising, working blind, but his instincts told him he was on the right track. He opened up a part of his mind to gather in every sign he could find of Adda-Leigh. His anxiety lifted as he realised that this was quite within his powers. His surface thoughts were now free to wander as they wished.

So Sam spoke into the howling wind, addressing the invisible presence of Father David. The dragon-boy was flying at ten thousand metres. But although his words were snatched away the moment they were uttered, Father David didn't seem to have any trouble hearing him.

'I suppose you've been working on some theories about what Master Richard might be up to?'

'Indeed I have.'

'You'd better tell me,' Sam said grimly.

THE FIREDRAKE CODEX

The voice of Father David spoke inside Sam's head.

'*We must look to history to understand the present, Sam. The Order of the Knights of the Pursuing Flame was founded in the twelfth century as a crusading order and they quickly became infamous for the zeal with which they slaughtered the non-Christian peoples they encountered in the Middle East, and on their various forays into the Balkans and Eastern Europe. This you know already.*

'*The Order's founder, and first Grand Master, Sir Bertrand De Loup, was said to have discovered a collection of mysterious prophecies in the Holy Land, bound together in a manuscript known as the Firedrake Codex. I do not know the true origin of these prophecies, but I tell you as a priest, there is nothing remotely holy about that book.*

'*In 1405 the Order fell into bitter dispute with the Papal* authorities, over unpaid tribute. The Pope declared the Order heretical in 1407 but, before they were dissolved, and their Grand Master burnt at the stake, they succeeded in spiriting away the vast fortune they had amassed through plunder, apparently hiding it on various tiny islands in the Aegean, the Mediterranean and the Baltic.

'The Order and its knights disappeared from history. But they did not cease to exist.

'In 1492, when the first Europeans arrived in the South China Sea, a Scandinavian priest named Vitas Jorgsen was head of the Christian mission that landed on the isolated Luhngdou Island. The Order had survived as a secret society, and Jorgsen was the Grand Master. This was the true beginning, Sam, of the war between the Order and the dragon-folk of Luhngdou.

'There was a reason why the Order came to Luhngdou, you see, and forced our ancestors into conflict. It was because of the Codex.'

'The what?'

'The book, Sam. Pay attention. The book of prophecies.'

'Have you read it?'

'No. But I know of its content. The Codex consists of a sequence of texts of varied origin and date. The oldest of these speaks of a time prior to the creation of heaven and earth, when angels and dragons rubbed shoulders in the presence of God. The Codex claims that when Lucifer began his rebellion against the Almighty, the dragons sided with the losers and were thrown down into Hell along with the fallen angels. After Lucifer had brought about the expulsion of man from Eden, the dragons frequented the world, mixing freely with the descendants of Adam and Eve. Conflict between man and dragon was inevitable and many were killed on both sides. And yet love and hate are often two sides of the same coin. Some dragons and humans intermarried and had children and their children had children and eventually the dragon blood was diluted and lost in the great sea of humanity. But in some humans the strain ran deep, and one such tribe settled on an island far to the east. Certain special members of this tribe were said to be born as ordinary human children, but, around their fourteenth year, they undergo a series of transformations, eventually becoming fully-fledged dragons, with many powers, both physical, mental and spiritual.'

'But that can't be true! I'm not some kind of a devil-child! What do our ancestors say? The Luhngdonese? They must have alternative myths and legends.'

'We know that to the Luhngdonese their dragon kin were friends and protectors, not monsters or devils. Alas, much of their lore is lost, Sam, and what little is left has mainly survived within the twisted teachings of the Order. As a priest of the Companions I studied much of this material, hoping to discover the truth behind the lies. The Luhngdonese cannot speak for themselves. They have been driven to the brink of extinction. There is only you and I left, as far as is known, with any Luhngdonese blood in our veins at all.'

'But why are you harping on about the Order? Aren't they gone, defeated, wiped out by the Companions?'

'That was what I believed, but now I am not so sure.'

Sam soared over banks of cloud, skimming through the misty strands. He let instinct guide him. He moved unerringly towards London, heading for his old home and the marshland on the edge of the city, the place that had first quickened the dragon blood in his veins. Inside Sam's head, Father David's voice droned on.

'The manuscript records a vision, which the first Grand Master was said to have had. An angel appeared and charged him with the task of raising an army to fight a secret war against the legendary dragon-folk. When the island of Luhng-dou was discovered, with its serpent temples and stories of youths turning into dragons, the Order was convinced they had found their true enemy at last. The war was supposed to last for five hundred years, ending in a final battle between a champion of the Order and the last of the dragon-folk. You are the last of your kind, Sam. You are what the Codex calls "The Golden Dragon of the East". But who is the champion of the Order? Who is the so-called "Silver Warrior of the West"?'

Father David paused for a moment. When he continued there was a trace of hesitancy in his voice. *'I have been much preoccupied by the past recently, in dreams and memories. When I was a young priest I witnessed what I thought was the final defeat of the Order. The Companions,* led by Richard Smith, destroyed the last redoubt of our enemies, an ancient fortress with an underground laboratory, in which they were said to have been working to create some kind of terrible weapon. The brutality of that operation led to my breaking from the Companions for good and so I gave little thought to the weapon the Order was supposed to have been developing. I assumed it to have been a special poison, or a chemical, perhaps, or some kind of seeking device designed to identify and track down anyone of Luhngdonese descent. It has occurred to me recently however that the weapon may, in fact, have been a person. The Silver Warrior of the West.'

'But you can't build a person!'

'Genetics, Sam. Test tube babies. Cloning. Though they may bring benefits to humanity, such things can also be the stuff of nightmares.'

'And Master Richard, where does he fit into all this? He's Master of the Companions, isn't he, the enemies of the Order?'

'I am beginning to wonder, Sam. As Richard Smith rose through the ranks, the Companions gradually altered. When I was a boy, the Companions' ethos was protective above all things. We were pledged to defend the dragon-folk from the ravages of the Order. But with Richard as Chief of Operations, an all-out offensive was launched. What further changes might he have wrought, now that he has styled himself Master of the Companions . . . ?'

Father David's voice trailed off into silence.

Sam could think of no response. He banked and slipped free of the air current he had been following. As he broke through the cloud he saw below him the winding Thames, with the streets of London spread out for miles on either side of the slow, dark river. He could sense Adda-Leigh's presence, somewhere in the city. Now he had to find her.

QUICKER

West Street was a fifteen-minute bus ride from Gun-powder Row. If the traffic was bad it was quicker to walk.

A column of vehicles inched forward then ground to a halt, belching diesel fumes into the air of the hot summer afternoon. The main road was clogged with lorries, buses and cars, their occupants gazing bleakly out through grime-smeared toughened glass.

Georgette walked quickly along the pavement. Aaron jogged behind her, struggling to keep up. Jaws was trotting skittishly at his side, casting nervous glances at the traffic, twisting on his leash and seem-ingly doing his best to trip Aaron up and send him sprawling on the ground.

'Does it matter if we're a bit late?! We'll be there in

half a minute at this rate!' There was a whining tone to Aaron's voice that grated on Georgette's nerves. 'And what if it isn't Sam at all?' he went on. 'What if it's some nutcase? You hear all sorts of nasty stories.' He called out again. 'Wait up a minute, George. I got a stitch!'

She gritted her teeth and quickened her pace. She could think of nothing except the latest text Aaron had received, just as school had ended. The dragon logo, she was convinced, had identified it as another of Sam's mysterious communications.

A — meet wst st tbe stn 3.45 - S , the text had said. Georgette was going to make sure they kept the appointment as close to the stated time as possible. Quite who or what they were going to meet though, she wasn't sure.

AT THE HALFWAY STATION

Crisp blinked and twitched and gripped the wheel of
the car until his knuckles whitened.

'I know you, don't I?' he said. Adda-Leigh made no
reply. Her throat was dry, parched by fear. Crisp nodded to himself compulsively. 'Yeah. I know you. And I
know who you are, too, sir.' He nodded at Ishmael in
the rear-view mirror but was careful not to look too
closely at him.

'Richard Smith, the Master, he explained it all,'
Crisp babbled on. 'Looks don't mean a thing, I know
that now. It's what's inside that counts.'

He turned and bared his teeth in a wild grimace
that Adda-Leigh realised was intended as a smile. 'I'm
not a racist any more, see? Skin and all that, it means
nothing. We humans have to stick together now. There's

monsters out there. They're the real enemy. The monsters. So if I kill you it won't be because you're not white. It'll be because you're friends with the monsters.' Crisp nodded his head again and again.

'Stop,' Ishmael said. While Crisp had been babbling on, Ishmael had been, casting around as if searching for something, paying no heed to the driver's words. 'Stop,' he repeated. Crisp hit the brakes. 'He is near. I'm sure of it.'

'He? You mean –' Crisp gripped the steering wheel even tighter. He craned his neck and peered through the windscreen, looking up at the sky.

'He's back there,' said Ishmael. 'Under the ground. I must return. I must face him at last.'

'Don't go!' said Adda-Leigh. Ishmael was terrifying, particularly now she'd seen his face, but with him she was, at least, on familiar ground. All she knew of Crisp was that he had once wanted to kill her.

Ishmael looked at Adda-Leigh. There was pain and sorrow in his gaze. And something else. Regret? He shook his head.

'You shall not be harmed,' he said.

The unfinished station where Adda-Leigh had been held prisoner lay halfway between West Street and Palmer's Ferry Station. She sat in the back of the car with her eyes streaming from the unaccustomed daylight, still trying to get to grips with the rapid change in her situation. Now that Ishmael had gone, this might be her best chance of escape.

She glanced out of the window. There were people everywhere, cars, buses, people on foot, people on pushbikes. All she had to do was call out. Surely her face had been in the papers. Missing: have you seen this girl?

'Keep your eyes facing forward.' There was menace in Crisp's unsteady tones. Adda-Leigh turned her head and looked fixedly at the seat in front of her.

Her heart was pounding. Had the days she'd spent locked in a sunless cell broken her spirit? Certainly this sudden change of routine had left her disorientated and numb with fear. She took a deep breath.

Her thoughts spun. Come on, girl! Don't lose this opportunity. This could be your only chance to get away. Don't lose it!

Ishmael stood uncertainly by the car, looking around him, trying to get his bearings. He seemed to be sniffing the air, like a predator searching for the scent of its prey. Crisp wound down the window. 'You'd best get going, sir.' Still, he wouldn't look at Ishmael. 'People have started to stare.'

Though she didn't dare look out of the window, Adda-Leigh thought that staring was quite likely, given Ishmael's startling appearance. His shadow disappeared from beside the car and he was gone. Adda-Leigh could only imagine the reaction of the onlookers as he made his way back along the road to the disused station.

The car pulled away at last. Crisp gave a sigh of relief.

'I know he's on the side of us humans,' he said. 'But he still looks like a monster to me.'

Adda-Leigh sat in the back seat, frozen with apprehension, her wits dull with fear. Where was she being taken?

The car came to a stop at a junction, traffic lights on red. Crisp groaned and pounded the wheel impatiently.

A car pulled up alongside them. Four young men were sprawled inside, two in the front and two in the back. Loud music was blaring from the car speakers, the thudding bass line sending vibrations buzzing through the chassis and down through the road itself. Adda-Leigh suddenly knew this might be her only chance of raising the alarm.

Closest to her was a youth in dark glasses, slouched in the front passenger seat. The window was wound right down and his bare arm was draped decorously over the car door. A plume of blue smoke rose from the cigarette he held in his hand.

She rapped on the window, hard. The young man raised his head. She saw the beginnings of a smug smile start to form around the corners of his mouth. An attractive young woman wanted his attention.

'No! Help me, you idiot!' Adda-Leigh screamed. 'For God's sake, HELP ME!' The young man's brows puckered with surprise and alarm. Then Adda-Leigh was thrown back against the seat as the car lurched violently forward.

Horns blared and cars skidded and swerved as they shot the lights. Adda-Leigh tried the car door, tugging at the handle, plucking desperately at the lock. She was quite prepared to throw herself out of the car, despite the terrible injuries that would cause her. But the doors were locked. She couldn't even wind down the window.

'Is that it?' Crisp laughed, a hollow, mirthless sound. 'Hardly the Great Escape was it?'

Adda-Leigh's despair subsided as a burst of anger swept through her. No. This wasn't over. Whatever he had in store for her, she wasn't going to make it easy for him. At the very next opportunity, she would make another bid for freedom. She could tolerate her confinement no longer. She clenched her teeth and glared defiantly into the rear-view mirror. But Crisp's eyes were now firmly fixed on the road ahead.

HARM

'Well done, Sam, you have made good time. With any luck you will have freed Adda-Leigh before your other friends arrive. I fear you made a mistake in calling them. It's best they do not see you. It would be . . . difficult for them. I don't know why you arranged to meet them in the first place. I'm always here, if you need any help.'

'You're just a voice in my head, remember?' Sam stood at the top of the spiral stairs. The stairs descended into darkness, but he would have little trouble seeing. He didn't mention his reasons for contacting Aaron, the fact that he was hoping to free Adda-Leigh and then slip away, leaving his old friend to complete the rescue. In truth, he didn't want any of them to see him.

Sam had hovered high above West Street. He'd hung

on the wind and let the current shift him eastwards. Somewhere far beneath him, his senses told him, he would find Adda-Leigh. She was deep underground. He'd let his instincts guide him to a way in. With eyes sharper than any hawk he'd surveyed the back street behind the entrance to the disused station. Then he'd dived, falling like a bolt of lightning, too quick for any chance observer to see properly.

Now Sam stood in the gloom of the unfinished station and let his senses drift ahead of him, down the spiral stairs, along the dusty passageways, down to the train track itself, seeking the presence of the girl whose features he had drawn so often, in the sand on the coast of Ireland.

Something was wrong.

'She's not here!' His voice was strangled, his throat tight with fear. All around him he felt the recent presence of Adda-Leigh. The darkness seemed to vibrate with an echo of her passing. He could almost see her form, like an outline of shimmering Adda-Leigh-shaped dust, hanging in the air. But she was here no more. The quality of stillness in the shadows of the stairway told him that. What had happened to her? She'd been taken away. Others had been here. Panic swept through him and he felt weak.

Father David had fallen silent.

'She's not here!' Sam repeated. 'But someone is!'

He felt fire burning in his throat. His anxiety for Adda-Leigh was turning to rage at her captors, sending adrenalin surging through his blood. He shivered.

Far below, someone was waiting. Someone who'd recently entered the building by another entrance. Sam had a very strong impression of this person's intentions, which broke over him like a wave. The feeling was so intense it made him stagger and hold onto the bare wall for support. The stranger below meant him harm. Terrible harm.

Georgette swallowed. Aaron was wrong. It wasn't that she felt no fear. It was more that she had stopped really caring what happened to her. It was a feeling that had been spreading through her for a long time now. Even before all the traumas that accompanied her friendship with Adda-Leigh, she now realised that the numbness had been there. True, she had been a well-behaved student, quiet and hardworking as recently as six months ago, but she had long felt detached, as if she were just going through the motions. The long months leading to her parents' separation and eventual divorce had started the process. Recent events had propelled her into a different world altogether.

At least now her life felt more honest. Adda-Leigh was her friend and she was going to find her. It was all she cared about. It was what allowed her to choke back the fear rising inside her, and walk through the broken door and into the darkened passageway beyond.

She came to a heavy ironwork shutter, the sort used to close off entrances and subways on the Underground. The barrier had been torn down. It sagged against the wall, a twisted heap of old iron. Enough light still filtered through from the open doorway behind her for Georgette to see that beyond the broken shutter there was a spiral staircase, leading down.

She stepped over the tangled remains of the shutter and moved to the top of the staircase.

'Addie?' She had meant to call out, to bellow her friend's name into the darkness. What had emerged was a croaky whisper. She cleared her throat to try again. But before she could speak, she saw it. A light.

From somewhere on the stairs below, an intermittent light glowed and then dimmed, glowed and then dimmed again.

'Adda-Leigh!'

The light vanished. Georgette started down the steps, keeping close to the wall, her palms pressed against the cold tiles, feet feeling for the edge of the next step.

'Addie! It's me, Georgette!' Her call echoed then died in the fusty darkness. She saw the light again, brighter this time, glowing and dimming, a flickering, soft light that faded in and out. This wasn't the flash of a torch. This light seemed more organic. It swelled in intensity before sinking back into the dark again. What was it?

'Adda-Leigh?' Her voice was a whisper again. The light was close now. And she could hear a sound, a rasping, scraping, burbling sound, unidentifiable and utterly terrifying.

With her arms spread out and her back pressed against the curving wall she descended another half-dozen steps. Then she saw it.

The thing lay on the stairs. It was shaped like a man, but it was much too tall, the body somehow longer than it should be, the hands and feet, all the proportions, were wrong.

Georgette heard a thin, despairing scream that hung on the air. Her hand flew to her mouth and she chewed frenziedly on her knuckles. The scream, she realised, had been hers. She was seized by a fit of trembling but she couldn't look away from the beast lying sprawled on the staircase.

The light came from the creature's mouth. The burbling sound was its laboured breathing and with each gasping breath it let out a sputtering of fire, the flame licking over rows of snaggled-teeth set in a protruding jaw. As it fought to inhale, the fire was extinguished, swallowed, drawn back into its throat before being expelled once more, with an effort that spoke of some internal agony.

Georgette recognised the beast. She had seen it once before, out on the marsh on the night the grey-haired woman had been murdered. It seemed altered, bigger, more powerful looking, except now it was clearly badly injured.

The creature opened its eyes and looked up at her. It made a noise, a deep guttural mumbling. It was trying to speak.

'Where is she?' Georgette said. 'Where's Adda-Leigh?' Her voice was a barely audible croak but the thing on the stairs heard her and tried to reply. Its voice was too slurred, too low and rumbling for Georgette to make out the words. The creature seemed to realise this. It bowed its head, and fell silent.

Then a voice spoke to Georgette. Like a conscious thought, only more insistent and very definitely external in origin. The voice spoke to her through her mind. She recognised who it was, though he only said three words. It was Sam Lim-Evans, the boy from school, that Adda-Leigh had liked, the boy who had gone missing six months ago. His voice sounded small and uncertain and wracked with pain.

'Georgette. Help me,' the voice said.

RETURN TO DARKNESS

Crisp drove fast, leaving Adda-Leigh to pound on the windows and gesture at startled drivers as they raced past, but never pausing to allow her time to pass on any intelligible message.

She was sure someone would call the police, but would the police be able to catch up with them? They had already changed cars three times. On each occasion Crisp would screech to a halt and abandon the vehicle in the middle of the road, then he would tear open an envelope containing the keys to a new getaway vehicle.

'The Master had it all planned out,' Crisp told her, proudly, as if she was likely to appreciate the efficiency of her own kidnappers. Dragging Adda-Leigh from one car to another, ignoring her yells and wild struggles, as well as the horrified stares of any passers-by, Crisp would speed away again before anyone had the chance to intervene. There was no sign of the police.

The last leg of the journey proved to be the worst. They had left the city behind them. Fields stretched away on both sides of the road. There was barely any traffic. Adda-Leigh, exhausted and despairing, listened for the sound of police sirens. She heard none. Crisp had somehow evaded all pursuit.

A car was parked in a lay-by beside a field of corn. The car's driver, a tall and burly sandy-headed man, was urinating against a tree on the edge of the field.

Crisp put his foot on the brakes.

'They told me to improvise for the last leg,' he said. 'Just in case.' He leapt out of the car. The sandy-haired man looked up.

Adda-Leigh banged her fists on the car window. 'HELP ME! PLEASE!' Her shouts were hoarse and cracked and it tore at her throat to cry out but she had to make herself heard. She rattled at the door handle.

Crisp opened the door of the parked car. The keys were in the ignition. Now the sandy-haired man came running towards them. 'Hoi!' the man roared. 'That's my car!' He was red in the face and ran with his fists raised. Crisp frowned and stepped forward to meet him. The sandy-haired man never faltered in his headlong charge. Crisp planted his feet firmly and waited.

At the last moment he stepped aside and hacked at the shins of the onrushing giant with his heavy-booted feet, sending his would-be attacker hurtling forward. The sandy-haired man crashed to the ground. He struck his head on the roadside kerbstone and lay still.

Crisp grinned nastily and wiped his hands on his trouser legs. In the car, Adda-Leigh let out a moan of despair and pounded her forehead against the window in frustration. Crisp unlocked the door, took her by the arm and dragged her out.

He frog-marched her to the rear of the car, opened the boot and, before Adda-Leigh had registered what was happening, he bundled her in. The door of the boot closed and, once again, she found herself imprisoned in darkness.

TAKEN AWAY

Sam's head buzzed. Father David's voice was speaking somewhere deep within his mind but again he couldn't make out the words. Georgette was crouching over him.

Somewhere above them was Aaron. Sam sensed Aaron's presence, recognised his old school friend. He smiled, in spite of the agony he was in. It seemed incredible that he and Aaron had once inhabited the same world, and more extraordinary still that they were about to meet again. Sam could tell that Aaron was moving cautiously towards the top of the spiral staircase.

'Where's Adda-Leigh?' Georgette said again.

The force of her emotions howled through Sam's consciousness like a keen wind. Anger, fear, guilt, loyalty and affection, all mixed into a heady cocktail. Sam groaned under the weight of her anxiety.

'If you've hurt her . . .'

He reeled beneath the force of her fury. 'No.' His voice was little more than a throaty grunt but he managed to form the word more or less intelligibly. He tried to speak to her telepathically again, but he was too weak. He forced himself to swallow the pool of molten fire that had risen, unbidden, to the back of this throat. Slowly and painfully, he whispered out the truth.

'She was here . . . but they've taken her . . .'

'Who? Do you know?'

'It's him. It must be. The Warrior.'

A shudder ran through Sam as he remembered the attack. He had sensed the approach of one who meant him harm. On the spiral stairs, they'd met. The encounter had been brief. For Sam it had been near disastrous.

The physical powers he was constantly developing had isolated him from the rest of humanity, but at the same time they had granted him a feeling of complete invulnerability. Now, even that had been taken away from him.

The stranger had come up the pitch-black stairs. Sam, able to see despite the absence of light, had found himself looking straight into his opponent's eyes. Here was someone with the same visual abilities as his own. There would be no hiding place in this darkness.

He had recognised the eyes, the same silver-blue as Master Richard's. And there was something else, an air of haunting familiarity that chilled him to the bone as he stared into the ravaged face of this youth whose mind and body were, he clearly sensed, just as contorted as Sam's own. But he had no time to ponder on what this sense of recognition might mean.

'Seekest thou to destroy me?' the boy with the silver eyes had said. Sam recalled the voice, quiet and solemn in tone, and the strange way he spoke. A great sword was cradled in his arms, the blade over a metre in length. Grasping the weapon two-handed, he had advanced on Sam. The look in his eyes was cold and pitiless.

IF ANYTHING ELSE HAPPENS

'George? I can't see a thing? Where are you, mate?' Aaron's voice broke in on Georgette's racing thoughts. He was somewhere on the stairs above. His trainers shuffled on the concrete.

'Here!' she called, and she heard him give a sigh of relief. He was close by.

'Aaron! I'm here!'

'Am I glad to hear your voice!' Aaron clattered down the pitch-dark steps. 'I left Jaws tied up at the top. I couldn't hack it for so long, being in the dark and all on me tod.'

'Big baby!' Georgette regretted her words the moment she uttered them. After all, Aaron had come to see if she was okay, hadn't he?

He didn't seem to mind, however, and only reacted

with a brief chuckle of unashamed agreement.

'Give me a hand,' said Georgette. 'We have to get him to the top of the stairs.'

'Eh? Who?'

'It's . . .' Georgette paused. The thing sprawled on the steps was Sam. She realised that Adda-Leigh had been right all along. Her friend had recognised him the moment she'd looked into his eyes. Georgette hadn't been willing to believe it. But now she knew it to be true, even though she had no idea how such a transformation could be possible. This thing was Sam. This was what he had become. But would Aaron be able to accept it?

'There's someone injured down here,' she said at last.

'Is it Adda-Leigh?'

'No.'

'Could be the kidnapper!' Aaron's voice was fearful.

'I don't think so. It's someone who was trying to help. Where are you?'

The darkness was complete.

'By the wall.' Aaron was close. 'Here, I'm stretching out my hand.'

'Got you. Now take his arm. There. Got it?'

'Yeah. Christ, what's he wearing? Some kind of weird leather jacket? It feels all lumpy.'

'Never mind that. Help me lift him.'

Georgette could never have lifted Sam alone, but with Aaron taking the bulk of the weight, they managed to stagger back up to the top of the spiral stairs and into the passageway with the broken-down shutter. There, Aaron collapsed on his knees coughing and groaning.

'He weighs a ton!' he said. The light from the ticket hall area dimly illuminated the passageway. Georgette heard Aaron gasp.

'Wait,' he said. He lifted a trembling finger and pointed. Scaly lumps and contusions covered Sam's body from foot to head. Muscle and sinew lay taught beneath the reptilian skin. Spines crowned his head. His fingers were long and tipped with curving claws. One hand was clutched to a terrible, glistening wound, a sword slash that cut across his body from chest to hip. The gaping flesh had already begun to knit, however. The wounded beast looked solemnly back at Aaron.

'Wait,' Aaron said again. He was breathless. 'That ain't right.' He collapsed on the ground in a dead faint.

'Aaron!' Georgette knelt beside him, shaking him by the shoulder.

'Leave him,' Sam said.

'I can't lift you without him,' Georgette said. 'And I need you to find Adda-Leigh.'

'Yes,' Sam said. 'I'll be okay in a minute, I think. But I can't stay here. The police are on their way. If they find me here . . . God knows what they'll think. If I can just go somewhere to rest for an hour or so.'

'An hour! We have to find Addie! How do you even know she's still alive?'

'She's alive. I'd know if she wasn't. Besides, I think it's me her kidnappers really want. I don't understand why yet, but Adda-Leigh was taken so that I would have to come here. She's just bait.'

Georgette looked at Sam. Now his speech had become a little clearer, and she found she could follow his low-pitched mumblings without too much difficulty. She felt a stab of anger.

'So,' she said, 'her getting kidnapped and held prisoner for weeks, and everything her family has gone through because of it, and everything I've gone through, all of that, it's your fault, is it?'

Sam blinked but said nothing.

'If you don't get her back in one piece, Sam Lim-Evans,' Georgette said. 'I don't care if you can fly and spit out fire, I'll track you down and I'll make sure you suffer!'

'If anything like that happens,' said Sam, his gruff voice trembling with desperate concern. 'If anything else happens to Adda-Leigh . . .' He faltered, unable to complete the phrase. He took a deep shuddering breath and fixed Georgette with his piercing gaze. 'You won't have to worry about revenge. I'll die if anything happens to her,' he said.

GOING TO CHURCH

Adda-Leigh was thrown around painfully as the car sped on, swerving around corners at high speed. The journey seemed to last an age. Hours passed. Finally the car juddered agonisingly over a wildly uneven surface. There was a crash of splintering wood and they skidded to a halt.

Huddled in a ball in the darkness of the trunk, Adda-Leigh groaned out loud. She was choking on petrol fumes, bruised all over, and trying desperately not to panic at the thought that the car might have crashed and be about to burst into flames.

She heard Crisp scramble out from behind the wheel.

'Too fast, too fast . . .' he was muttering to himself. His footsteps rang out sharply with a curious echo. The boot was flung open.

'Get out!'

Adda-Leigh raised her head, blinking in the light. She rubbed her eyes and looked around her, stupefied by what she saw. They were inside a large church. The west doorway and the double doors leading in from the vestibule had both been smashed open. Tyre marks ran across the stone floor of the nave, all the way up the aisle. Crisp had driven right up to the altar, where his car had slewed to a halt, knocking over the front pew, splitting the dark-stained wooden seating.

'I said, get out!' Crisp grabbed Adda-Leigh by the arm and dragged her out of the boot.

'Where have you taken me? What is this place?' The church interior was stark and bare, the air musty with damp. There was a feeling of desolation. Adda-Leigh guessed this church hadn't seen a congregation or a service for some time. Crisp was agitated. He tugged at her arm and she stumbled along beside him. They passed through the shattered doorway and out into the vestibule.

A tall man with long white hair was standing silently with his arms folded across his chest. Crisp jumped when he saw the man.

'Master! I didn't know — I thought I'd got here before you — I mean . . .' Crisp stammered into silence under the withering glare of the pale-eyed man.

'Crisp. This is a low-key operation. I provide you

with a range of vehicles. You had no need to stop for petrol or to worry about being apprehended. All you had to do was quietly acquire a fourth car and bring the prisoner here in it. That shouldn't have been a problem for a man of your experience. But first you allow Ishmael to set off on a lone mission instead of sticking to the plan. Then you decide to half-kill a motorist, steal his car and drive it at top speed into this church. A half-trained ape could have made a better job of it than you!'

Crisp gaped. 'How did you know?'

The Master stepped forward and without a moment's hesitation struck Crisp hard across the face with the back of his hand.

'I have many eyes. You'd better pray that my contact in the local police can put enough obstacles in the way of anyone who might feel it their duty to follow the blundering trail you've left for all to see! If anything is allowed to interrupt the forthcoming ceremony then I shall hold you personally responsible.'

Crisp had sunk to his knees under the force of this verbal attack. He threw himself on the flagstones.

'Master! I'm sorry. I was so afraid. I thought the monsters were coming. I had to drive fast. I had to!'

'Silence!'

The Master turned his silver-blue eyes on Adda-Leigh. His lip curled in a contemptuous sneer. He pointed, as if any speech directed at her would be a waste of breath. There was a low wooden door in the wall, a door that led to the church tower, Adda-Leigh guessed. A key was in the lock and the door stood half open.

Another prison. Adda-Leigh gave a compulsive shake of her head and ran. The Master was too quick for her. He moved with a dancer's grace, but with the violent speed of a fox pouncing on a rabbit. He had his back to the outside door before Adda-Leigh was even halfway there.

He took a step towards her.

'Okay! Okay!' Adda-Leigh backed through the low wooden door into the tower. She'd seen him strike Crisp and didn't want to risk being on the receiving end of this man's blows.

She backed into a roughly plastered wall. The door slammed in her face and she heard the key turn in the lock.

UNDER THE BAR

Sam was listening to Father David. He was deliberately not thinking about Adda-Leigh.

He would find her with telepathy. Soon, he would make contact with her again, the girl he'd dreamed about in Ireland for so many months. But he knew instinctively that he had to let his wound heal before he tried to use his psychic powers again. Too much strain on his reserves of energy and he might face total collapse.

'You're sure Aaron only fainted?'

Sam sighed. 'Yes! For an imaginary friend, you worry too much! Aaron'll be fine.' He ignored the stab of guilt he felt at leaving his old friend behind in the unused station. Aaron would get into trouble with the Transport Police, that was certain. They'd heard the sirens as they'd slipped away. Security was a very sensitive area these days. Whatever Aaron told the police was unlikely to be believed. That would probably annoy them even further. But if Sam and Georgette had tried to take him with them they might all have been caught. In the end, Aaron would be dismissed as a stupid but well-meaning kid, who'd set off a security alert when he went looking for his missing schoolmate. Leaving him had been the best course of action. But it was still a harsh thing to have done.

Sam lay on his back underneath the rickety wooden staircase. The cellar still stank of stale beer, even though the Ferryman's Arms had been closed for weeks. Empty barrels filled much of the space beyond the staircase. The ceiling was low; Sam would have to bend double to move around. But he lay still. The sword wound needed a little more time to heal properly.

A livid scar now ran the full length of his body, rather than an open wound. The journey from West Street to the old pub by the canal had set back the healing process somewhat, but he was making up lost time. Beneath the skin, layers of muscle were rapidly knitting together. Soon he would be ready.

He lay with his head resting on a mouldering bag of old cricket equipment, left behind by some long-disbanded pub team. It was uncomfortable, but not bad enough to force him to move.

'What about the dog?'

Jaws the Alsatian was stretched out beside Sam on the cellar floor. The dog's muzzle was resting against the boy's scale-encrusted leg. Sam reached out and scratched Jaws delicately under the chin. Jaws's tail thumped the ground in a display of devoted appreciation.

'I told you. I've met him before. Out on the marsh. He startled me then. I didn't mean to, but I must have done something bad to his mind. His nerve was gone. He was afraid of everything. Now I've made him better. He's not afraid. In fact, he's totally fearless.'

'Your powers of psychic healing are still very erratic, Sam. You must be careful! You don't know what effect your meddling might have on this poor creature.'

'Well, he seems a lot happier now than when I found him. He looked like he was going to chew his own foot off he was so scared!'

'You are sure Aaron was breathing when you left him?'

'YES! And before you ask, no one saw me on the way here. Though why it really matters I don't know.'

'You have to be responsible about these things, Sam. Think of how Aaron reacted when he saw you!'

'Well, Aaron is Aaron. But don't worry, I went through back gardens most of the way, and I took it slow. May have startled a few cats, but that's about it. Georgette let me in. Her dad's out.' Sam paused and gazed up at the rough wooden boards that were a ceiling in the cellar, but the floor of the old bar above. 'My father used to come to this pub, when it was still open. It was his local. He used to wheel himself in, in his chair, and then get the bar staff to wheel him home again eight pints later. God, he was a mess!'

'Sam.' Father David's voice was hesitant. '*I fear I know who it was that attacked you in the Underground. I don't know if you are ready to face him yet.*'

'I don't have a choice. They have Adda-Leigh.' There was a note of finality in Sam's voice. 'And I already know who it was. It was the Order's secret weapon.'

'*The Silver Warrior of the West!*'

'Yeah. Him.'

'*How could you be sure?*'

'It was in his eyes, I think. I just knew. He didn't look too good. Something wrong with his face.'

'*Scars? Sickness? Premature ageing? The Order's cloning techniques must have had their downside. Don't let appearances fool you.*'

'I won't. He was as strong as I am. Stronger, maybe. He could have killed me.'

Father David was silent for a moment. Then he spoke up again, his voice betraying a somewhat forced manner.

'*So the Master of the Companions and the Silver Warrior have thrown in their lot together! What can this mean?*'

Before Father David could launch into any further hypothesising the cellar door opened and Sam heard Georgette's footstep on the stairs.

He struggled to sit up. The pain from his wound was much less now.

'Have you had enough rest?' Georgette said. Sam could see she had to struggle to contain her horror at the sight of him.

'I'm okay.' He spoke tersely. The revulsion she felt was painful to recognise.

'Then it's time to find Adda-Leigh. You know where they've taken her?'

'All I have to do is think about her. I'll be able to follow. But –'

'Come on then. What are we waiting for?'

'We? I can't take you, Georgette!'

'Why not? You're sure to need some back up. And looking the way you do must surely have its limitations.'

'Because people want to run screaming at the sight of me, you mean?'

She said nothing.

'All right. But we'll be flying. You might find it a bit . . .'

'I'll be fine.' Georgette interrupted him. She folded her arms and gave him a look that brooked no argument.

Sam looked at her. He hadn't expected this. Freeing Adda-Leigh on his own would make sense. But there was still the fear at the back of his mind that she too would be sickened at the sight of him. He couldn't leave her alone to make her own way home once he'd released her. Who knows what sort of shape she'd be in? If her friend was there too, Georgette could take care of her while he slunk away into the shadows.

'Okay.' Sam shrugged and dragged a length of old rope out from underneath the cricket bag.

'Help me untangle this,' he said. 'You'll need something to hold on to. Jaws can follow from down on the ground.'

'You were going to take the dog, but not me?' Georgette said.

This time, it was Sam who made no reply.

Some ten minutes later Sam stood on the deserted canal towpath. Georgette had wound the rope firmly around her arms and her waist and she was tied tightly on Sam's back. Sam had wrapped a length of heavy tarpaulin they'd found in the bar cellar around his body to protect Georgette from the jagged scales of his skin. Both her arms were clasped around him and she was clinging on tightly, even though they hadn't yet left the ground. He was aware of her pounding heart and the numbing fear she was feeling for what they were about to do. But she was going to do it anyway, fly through the sky roped to the back of an impossible creature, half-boy half-dragon. He was suddenly glad she was coming with him.

'God, you're brave, Georgette.' He muttered the words, embarrassed at the baldness of the compliment.

'Shut up and fly!' she said, speaking through gritted teeth. Sam felt her gulp down a shuddering breath, preparing herself for the shock of flight. He kicked off with both feet, spread his wings, and flew straight up into the hazy evening sky.

SIDES

Adda-Leigh was in a narrow gallery below the tower and above the vestibule. A staircase led up from the locked door below. As she'd climbed the stairs, telling herself if she never climbed another spiral staircase in her life it'd be too soon, she had passed a loophole window, the sort originally designed for shooting arrows through. It was too narrow to climb out, even if she could have broken the glass that now sealed it up, but at least it offered a view.

She was in an old church, somewhere in the countryside. A narrow lane flanked by hedgerows ran past the front of the building. Adda-Leigh watched for ten minutes but no cars passed along it. The nearest dwelling was a farmhouse on the far side of a field of vivid green cabbages. The house looked empty.

Adda-Leigh could only hope there were more houses on the other side of the church, where she couldn't see. If not, it seemed she had been taken to a place where, like her previous prison, she could scream and yell all she wanted but no one would ever hear her.

The stairs led up to the belfry itself, but the door to it was locked. Adda-Leigh had peered through the broad cracks in the wooden door and seen the bells. The largest looked to be as tall as she was. If she could get into the belfry, or the room beneath it where the bell ropes were hanging, she could raise the alarm by sounding a peel on the bells. But despite the cracks, the oak-panelled doors were all too strong for her to break down.

So she'd found her way onto the gallery. It struck her that the Master must have known where she could and couldn't get to. He showed no surprise when he glanced up from the nave and saw her on the stone balcony. He turned away with a look of disdain on his face. It was obvious he didn't believe Adda-Leigh represented any kind of threat at all. He saw her presence as no more significant than that of a stray pigeon, or a church mouse.

Adda-Leigh glared down at the Master. She ached all over. Weeks of fear and anxiety, lack of fresh air and exercise, and the recent violent shaking she had endured in the boot of the speeding car had left her feeling drained of all strength. And now, once again, her captors seemed to have her trapped. She ground her teeth and looked out between the carved stone columns. There had to be a way out. She refused to be beaten. And yet she could think of no way to succeed.

There was a newcomer down in the nave. Adda-Leigh heard no footsteps in the vestibule, nor any sound of approach, but suddenly Ishmael was there, standing at the Master's shoulder.

The youth wiped a bead of sweat from his hairless head and laid a lengthy object wrapped in cloth down upon the altar.

'You fought him?' The Master's eyes flashed with concern.

Ishmael nodded.

'And is it over?'

This time Ishmael shook his head.

'He lives, as do I.'

'You escaped without any . . . difficulties?'

'I did.'

'You have arrived quicker than I anticipated. And he will follow you, this I know. If not for the love of battle then for the girl.'

'She is here?'

The Master gave a dismissive nod. 'He will track her down. And the others are on their way. Your great battle will not pass without an appropriate witness. So how went your skirmish with the boy-dragon?'

'I smote him down, Master. But he is strong. He has the flames of Hell to protect him.' Ishmael held up one hand. Adda-Leigh saw that the flesh was raw red, the charred skin tightly stretched over the bones.

The Master glanced at Ishmael's injury. 'It will heal soon,' he said. 'But do not underestimate your foe. Fire could make an end of you, if you allow it to.'

Ishmael was looking at the car blocking the aisle of the church, as if he had only just noticed it.

'You have driven a car into the church, desecrating holy ground?' His voice was full of alarm. 'Surely the Almighty will . . .'

The Master interrupted him. 'The Almighty will forgive the fool who was responsible, though I may not. Just as he will forgive you your impetuous attack on your enemy before the appointed hour. Never forget, Ishmael, God is on our side. And our God is not the namby-pamby purveyor of peace and love that certain limp-souled churchgoers pray to. He is a vengeful God, a jealous God, a God of war!'

The Master paced back and forth across the flagstones. His voice rose, echoing dramatically around the vaulted ceiling of the old church. 'To counter the fires of Satan, he forges cold steel! He arms his Silver Warrior with all the powers of science! We are the true knights of God, and you, Ishmael, are our champion! From the laboratories of the Order, you have sprung, born – nay, created – to slaughter the last of the cursed, God-defiling dragon-folk of Luhngdou!'

Trembling, Ishmael fell to his knees and bent his head, overcome by emotion. The Master laid his hand on the youth's broad shoulder. 'Arise, Ishmael. We must prepare. An ancient prophecy is about to be fulfilled. The hour of the final battle is at hand!'

BLIND FLIGHT

The rope held Georgette secure, but still she clung to Sam's back, her eyes closed against the buffeting winds, against the horrifying drop to the earth spread out below them, and against the vastness of the heavens above them.

Her face was pressed against the tarpaulin that protected her from the vicious texture of the skin on Sam's back. It wasn't like the skin of any living creature she'd come across before. Cold scales and hardened blisters, a texture like a barnacle encrusted rock. Despite the tarpaulin, she could still feel the movement of the muscles beneath the skin as he dragged himself across the skies with the rhythmic and powerful strokes of his wings. Sam was real and this was really happening.

Georgette felt her stomach leap and churn as they slipped down and down, circling, riding on the currents of air, hundreds of metres above the ground.

BLIND LOVE

As he flew, Sam let his mind empty and then allowed all his memories of Adda-Leigh to pour in and fill it up. He recalled her long face, like a delicate carving, the colour of her skin, like polished wood, her long-fingered hands, always moving as she spoke. Once again he saw her standing on the doorstep of his flat in Marshside. He couldn't turn the keys in the lock because his hands were so cold. He'd been out on the marsh. The change had already started. Ever since he'd first known her, he'd been altered, no longer quite human. She knew that, didn't she?

He had to rescue her. That much was clear and straightforward. Master Richard knew that. So did the other one, the one that had attacked him. Sam knew he was flying into a trap, but he knew he had no choice.

What was uncertain was how Adda-Leigh would react when she saw him. He didn't doubt his ability to try to save her. But talking to her afterwards, just an ordinary conversation with a girl he liked, something he yearned for helplessly, that was a much more difficult prospect.

And so he still avoided any attempt to contact her telepathically. He'd managed to speak directly to Georgette's mind when she found him in the tunnel, so presumably he would be able to communicate with Adda-Leigh the same way. But what would he say? What would she think? Instead he concentrated on locating her, focusing his mind on her presence, Adda-Leigh as a physical mass, a collection of atoms taking up a certain area on the surface of the planet. This time, he couldn't afford to make a mistake.

His wing-beats followed his flowing thoughts, hom-ing in on her at a level somewhere below conscious-ness. He found Adda-Leigh, far beyond London, miles from any city, and her presence drew him towards her. He flew blind, spiralling down through the clouds towards the girl locked in the church. Like Georgette, roped to his back, and who Sam had forgotten was even there at all, he was flying with both eyes tightly closed.

THE FREEDOM OF THE ROAD

Adda-Leigh looked out across the nave, past the stolen car, to the altar, where Ishmael and the Master stood, their backs to the gallery. She looked down at the first row of pews directly below her. The architecture of the church interior, with its stone columns, carved capitals and moulded archways, all provided ample hand and foot holds to allow a bold climber to scramble down to the floor. But could she make the climb in silence, so as not to alert the two men standing at the other end of the church? And if she slipped and fell, the flagstones and dark-stained wooden pews would shatter her bones, leaving her crippled, if not dead.

But who knew how much longer the Master would allow her to live anyway? The chances of success were slim, but she didn't hesitate. She swung one leg over the balustrade, then the other.

She sat for a moment, watching Ishmael and the Master for any signs they were aware of her intentions. Down by the altar, Ishmael was on his knees again. He was holding up a sword, its blade laid across the palms of his hands, his arms outstretched. The Master stood over him, a hand resting lightly on the youth's shoulder. It was a gesture of ownership, like a man with a savage but obedient dog, reaching down and touching its collar. The setting sun was pouring crimson light through the west doors and through the stained glass window behind the gallery. The blade of Ishmael's sword shimmered and blinked, burning with blood-red fire.

Adda-Leigh fought off the shiver of fear that ran through her. She turned to face the stonework, took firm hold with both hands and lowered herself into space.

From the far end of the church she could hear the Master's voice intoning majestically. Adda-Leigh concentrated on the descent; her sweating hands clasping the cold stone, her feet feeling for the next stone ledge or relief carving. The Master's voice floated through the still air of the empty church. He spoke of duty and sacrifice and of the glory of the Silver Warrior of the West. Whether he was saying a prayer or delivering an eve of battle speech, she couldn't tell. With the Master, she thought, there probably wasn't much difference between the two.

When she was as near to the ground as she could get, Adda-Leigh jumped. It was a drop of about three metres, but she hit the flagstones hard and felt her ankle twist under her. A hot spurt of pain shot up her leg but still she ran for the open west doors, ran into the blinding light of the dying sun.

She heard them coming after her and she knew it was hopeless but still she dragged her injured foot behind her, hobbling and hopping, throwing herself forward, fleeing desperately into the open air, into the last of the daylight.

She fell before she reached the road, but continued to crawl across the swathe of sandy gravel in front of the church. She heard the crunch of footsteps. Then the Master and Ishmael were there, standing over her. She ignored them, her eyes fixed on the road in front of her. The road, escape, freedom. She crawled on.

'Leave her.' The Master's voice was filled with a barely contained delight.

'But, Master, she's hurt.' Ishmael's voice was unsteady. 'Her ankle may be broken. We must help her.'

'She has served her purpose. Look.'

Adda-Leigh crawled away from them. They didn't

follow. She hauled herself upright and sat with her hands raised to the sky. She was caked in dust. Blood oozed through the yellow dust that covered her torn palms. Her ears were ringing and her entire body was suffused with pain. But she had made it to the road. She looked up.

The western sky was still soaked in red light but the sun had disappeared below the horizon. A dark shape was approaching, flying, silhouetted against the banks of crimson cloud. A shape somewhat like a human figure, its head thrust forward, legs trailing behind and, at its shoulders, a pair of powerful wings steadily beating the air.

FOUND

Georgette beat her fists against Sam's flanks. He seemed oblivious to her, but she couldn't undo the ropes herself. She was helpless, tied to his back, forgotten. He stood on the grassy verge, across the road from the church. Georgette couldn't see over his shoulder properly. She didn't know what was going on.

'Let me down, Sam!' She kicked at the backs of his legs. He must have noticed her at last because he slipped the claw of one finger beneath the tightly wound rope and cut through the makeshift harness as easily as if he were snapping a single thread. He reached behind him with his other hand and lowered Georgette to the ground, like a schoolboy sloughing off his backpack. The tarpaulin slithered down and lay crumpled in the dust. Sam kicked it away from him.

Georgette stood, swaying dizzily in the long, dry grass, trying to regain her balance after the disorientating flight. Sam was between her and the church. Without seeming to so much as tense his muscles, he sprang up, beating the air with the tips of his wings, and hovered above the empty road. Georgette saw a broad-shouldered figure outside the church. A man with strange puckered features, somehow both old and young. He looked up at Sam, his expression full of ardent sorrow. Behind him, another man, with long white hair, hurried into the church through broken porch doors.

The windows either side of the porch were boarded up. Weeds were sprouting through the gravel. Georgette could see this church was not currently in use.

The old/young man spoke. 'Hast thou found me, o mine enemy?' he said to Sam.

Sam, still hovering in the air, made no reply. The two of them stared at each other, neither willing to break the gaze.

It was then that Georgette noticed there was someone in the road, sprawled there, half-sitting, half-lying in the dirt at the edge of the tarmac. With a jolt of shock, Georgette realised who it was. Her face was thin and drawn. She was covered in scratches, coated in yellow dust. Her eyes were red-rimmed and blood-shot. But it was her. It was Adda-Leigh. And she was alive. And Georgette had found her at last.

DRAGON-KIN

Sam looked upon his enemy. What was it about this raddled youth that Sam found so chillingly familiar? He had eyes like Master Richard, but that wasn't all. There was something else.

'Ishmael!' Master Richard came striding out of the church, his boots crunched on the gravel. He held the long sword, the same blade that had wounded Sam before. This was what Ishmael had brought, wrapped in cloth, all the way from his underground hideout. The Master tossed it up into the air. Without looking round, Ishmael lifted one arm, opened his hand and then closed his fist around the hilt of the sword. The scar on Sam's torso throbbed with pain as he watched a glimmer of reflected light running across the length of the blue-metal blade. He knew then, with a frightening certainty, that this sword could kill him.

'Sam! Be careful! You're in great danger!'

Sam didn't reply. He realised he had to face the coming encounter alone. The priest's voice continued speaking in urgent tones, but Sam stopped listening.

Master Richard took a step back. He still held something in his hands. It was the rack of Chinese gods, the Five Generals, which Sam had last seen in the cottage over in Ireland. Georgette had crossed the road and was helping Adda-Leigh to her feet. The two girls were safe, Sam thought, as long as he kept Ishmael and Master Richard busy. He had to give them what they wanted. But what did they want? A thousand questions crowded into Sam's head.

'Why?' he said at last. His voice broke the stillness of the evening air. Far in the distance there was traffic, a dog barking, the evening chorus of roosting birds, but around the church there hung a pall of silence. No birds sang here.

'Why?' Sam repeated. He drifted on the cooling air, moving a little closer to Ishmael, whose eyes never left his. It was Master Richard who spoke.

'We needed you here and we knew you would come. No self-control. Your pathetic schoolboy crush led you like a bull by the nose.'

'But you were with me in Ireland. If you wanted me dead, why not just kill me then?'

'Oh, but I don't want you dead, Sam,' said Master Richard. 'At least, not until you've fought. Don't you see? The fight is everything! The Silver Warrior of the West and the Golden Dragon of the East, you must fight, and then the prophecy shall be fulfilled! What good would it do for Ishmael here to sweep off your head in one swift, merciful blow? That's not a battle, that's merely an execution! I had to meet you myself, to get rid of that fool priest who thought he'd saved you. I tested you Sam, and found you wanting.'

Master Richard paced the gravel, puffs of dust rising around his boots as he spoke.

'In less enlightened times the people around these parts would entertain themselves with blood sports, bear baiting, bull baiting, dog-fights. Those dumb animals needed to be goaded into aggression. You, Sam, are one such animal. You have become less than human; you have to be brought to fighting pitch, artificially, if you are to stand any chance against our superhuman champion!'

Ishmael stood still and silent, the broadsword held steady, its tip pointing at Sam's heart. Sam looked at him.

'Who are you?' he said. Ishmael made no reply. Master Richard laughed.

'Father David was a soft-hearted fool. He smuggled a child out of the ruins of the Order's last bastion. It was there that the Order's scientists had worked on an ongoing project to raise the perfect warrior, the ultimate champion. That was the child your priest saved. He did me a favour. You see, despite what you know of me I am, and always have been, like Ishmael, a servant of the Order. Like Ishmael, I was raised from childhood with a single mission in mind. Infiltrate the Companions, rise through their ranks, establish a network of turncoats and agents throughout their ranks and then, when the time was ripe, purge the Companions of their old guard. A masterstroke! The Order found they could not defeat the Companions, so they resolved to become them instead! Of course, some, like the Grand Master, were against the plan. They paid the ultimate price. But for those that chose to follow my lead, and support the Silver Warrior of the West, glory awaits.

'I returned to the Balkans and tracked Ishmael down. His surrogate family joined the ranks of the dead, just more victims of the civil war, as far as anyone knew. And Ishmael became my pupil, training every moment of his life, for this one final encounter. You ask me who he is? He is the link between you and I, Sam. Engendered in a laboratory test-tube, gestated in an artificial womb, his blood strengthened with samples of my own DNA and also that of your dragon-kin, provided by your own great-grandmother, a loyal servant of the Order and a traitor to her own kind! Ishmael is the closest I will ever come to having a son, and the closest you will ever come to having a brother. And now, at my bidding, he is going to destroy you!'

IN TURMOIL

Adda-Leigh allowed Georgette to lead her away into the cornfield on the far side of the church. Her ankle was swollen now, and she couldn't bear to put any weight on it. She had to lean heavily on Georgette's bony shoulder. Georgette held her arm.

'You're so thin!'

'I've been on a diet, girl!' Adda-Leigh said. She remembered the soup Ishmael had brought her every day, down in her underground cell. She felt light-headed. She started to giggle hysterically but her chest hurt and she forced herself to stop. Georgette looked at her, frowning with concern.

'No further,' said Adda-Leigh. 'I have to sit down.'

There were no houses nearby, just a scattering of farm buildings out across the fields. There were no lights burning in any of them, although the dusk was now thickening into full darkness. The nearest sign of life looked to be at least fifteen minutes' walk away.

'We have to get help! Where is this place? Why are there no houses?' Georgette glanced around frantically. 'I can't believe there're no houses! Why build a church where there aren't any houses? What kind of a congregation do they get here? Scarecrows and rabbits?'

Adda-Leigh giggled again. Then she moaned and put a hand to her chest.

'Georgette, I have to sit down.'

'Okay. We can hide in the field. Nobody saw us come in here. I don't think they're interested in you, now that . . . he's here.'

Adda-Leigh put her arm around Georgette's back and together they waded into the corn. The stalks rustled and crackled as they pushed on into the field. A few metres in Adda-Leigh sank to the ground and Georgette crouched down beside her.

'It is Sam, isn't it?' said Adda-Leigh. The last time she'd seen him he'd looked like a melancholy boy trapped in a dragon-skin. But the changes were deeper now. The boy who'd been in her art class at school, who she'd tried to get to know, back before his disappearance, he was now an even more distant memory. What was left to recognise?

She looked out through the curtain of cornstalks and

stared at the creature that had once been Sam, hovering in the air in front of the church. Back in her cell in the Underground, she'd longed for him to fly to her rescue. Now that he had, the reality of his condition was truly shocking. Their only previous encounters since his transformation had taken hold had been brief and dreamlike. What would it be like to try to talk to him, again?

Adda-Leigh suppressed another fit of giggling. Her nerves were gone, at last. 'What do you think's going on?' she said.

'They're going to fight. That's what this has all been about. You were just bait, to bring Sam here, to make him fight.'

'Why? Who are they?'

Georgette looked at her. 'I thought you'd know,' she said.

'Not me, I'm just a kidnap victim. Nobody tells me anything.' There was bitterness in her voice.

'The police are looking for you. You'll need to go to hospital.' Georgette looked at her. It was dark now, but Adda-Leigh could still just about make out Georgette's eyes, wide with anxiety.

'Are you all right, Addie? Did they hurt you, or anything . . .?' She trailed off.

'Don't worry. I'm okay, apart from this ankle, and that was my fault. The white-haired man is really scary but Ishmael isn't too bad.'

Georgette shuddered. 'He looks like nothing on earth. How did you bear it?'

Adda-Leigh shrugged. 'I was tricked. A note came for me, telling me to go to some old warehouse up behind Glass Street. I thought it was from Sam.' Adda-Leigh fell silent.

'You should have told me where you were going,' Georgette said, 'or told your mum, or someone. At least we'd have known where to start looking.' Now there was a trace of bitterness in Georgette's tone. Was she angry with her? Adda-Leigh wondered. But this was not the time to work such things out. Something was happening by the church.

'Look,' Georgette said. 'Who's this?'

CIRCLING

The sound of an engine and the swish of tyres turning on the unmade road filled the air. A coach slowed to a halt outside the church.

Adda-Leigh groaned. 'Look's like they've got reinforcements.'

From the door at the front of the coach, Crisp jumped down onto the gravel forecourt. He stood holding the door.

'Him!' Georgette stared at Crisp.

'Yeah, he brought me here, but he's not in charge. The one with the white hair must have sent him out to give this coach party directions.'

'Look at Sam. What's he doing?'

'He's come to rescue me,' Adda-Leigh said. 'I knew he would. He's just come a bit late, that's all. I got out on my own.'

Georgette watched as Sam folded his wings and dropped to earth like a stone. The three figures in front of the church were silhouetted against the indigo sky. They circled each other cautiously, their total silence preserving the stillness of the night around them.

Behind them a group of figures disembarked from the coach. Men in expensive suits or well-cut uniforms. Business leaders, politicians, army officers and senior policemen. Nine of them, altogether. They took up position in front of the church, for all the world like a group of well-to-do tourists dutifully come to view a site of historic interest.

Georgette swallowed. She had no real idea what was happening outside the church but it was clearly a matter of life and death. What if Sam lost? What if the white-haired man and the other one, the one with the sword, and Crisp and the nine men from the coach, what if they overpowered Sam and killed him? He'd been badly injured when Aaron and Georgette found him. There was no reason to think he was indestructible. And if he lost the fight his killers would come looking for Georgette and Adda-Leigh. They'd be hunted through the corn, like animals.

'We have to get away.' She tugged at Adda-Leigh's sleeve. The garment was crisp with dirt. Adda-Leigh had been wearing the same clothes ever since she'd been taken.

'I can't. My ankle. It hurts.' Adda-Leigh's gaze was riveted on the conflict building by the west door of the church.

'Then I'll go. There's a light out there — across the next field. There'll be a house, with a phone. I'll call the police.'

But Adda-Leigh grabbed Georgette by the arm, her long fingers digging into her skin. 'Don't leave me!'

She must be in shock, Georgette realised. One minute she was giggling, the next she was terrified. There was nothing to be done. How could she leave Adda-Leigh on her own, in the state she was in? They would have to wait and watch, and hope that, whatever mysterious reasons might lie behind the fight unfolding before them, it would be Sam who would prevail. If not, it might spell the end for all of them.

BLOOD BROTHERS

Knees bent, feet together, Sam hit the gravel. Tiny stones flew out in all directions. A puff of yellow dust billowed up around his clawed toes, like a miniature mushroom cloud rising about a tiny desert test zone. Everything was clear and vivid. He heard his breathing, the beating of his heart, the rush of his blood. He heard the breath of his adversaries, and their hearts pounding in their chests, and their blood, circulating through veins and arteries, feeding the cells, nourishing the bodies. And here they were, circling one another, set on spilling that blood into the dust.

'Fight me if you must,' Sam said. His voice cracked as he spoke, and caught in his throat, making his words sound ridiculous. 'But let the girls go.'

Master Richard shook his head. 'I can't abide untidiness,' he said.

Sam let his thoughts float free, like background noise. His instincts were now in control. He heard the nine men from the coach shifting their weight in the gravel as they stood in a line behind him, watching. Their whispers carried on the air.

'I say, it's very impressive isn't it?'

'Good old Richard. The man knows how to put on a show, you have to hand it to him.'

'A show? This is for real! Don't you see! The Codex. The prophecies! All of it real!'

'Steady on. Prosthetics, surely? Animatronics. Wire work. Mirrors. Top of the range stuff. Very expensive. But, real? Surely not.'

These men, whoever they were, didn't seem to be a threat. So Sam watched Ishmael and the Master, locked all six senses on them, waiting for the faintest of warning signs, some split-second tensing of muscle or spark of mental activity that would tell him if either of them were about to strike.

Ishmael, he could tell, was doing the same. Elements of the same blood coursed through their veins. At a surface level it had affected them differently, but their kinship was deep and indisputable. Sam had felt it the moment he first encountered this Silver Warrior, champion of the Order of the Knights of the Pursuing

Flame. What the Master had said was true. They were brothers. Dragon and anti-dragon. Opposites. One the mirror of the other. But brothers nonetheless.

The Master himself was a wild card. He didn't have the powers that Sam and Ishmael possessed, but his intentions were obscure, his actions unpredictable. He'd been deceiving Sam, manipulating his every decision since he'd first found him in the ruined house in the Irish woodland.

'The moment has arrived.' Master Richard raised his voice, addressing the line of men from the coach, who were watching proceedings with a mixture of emotions ranging from mild interest to sheer terror and hopeless awe. The Master's normally steady voice trembled with emotion. 'Here, in this place, the site of the first church the Order built on this island of Britain, here, where an unnamed knight put the last of the British dragon-folk to the slaughter, it has fallen to me, the first Grand Master of the Companions, the new Order, to arrange and participate in this, the final battle. And for you nine, representatives of the group of moles and agents whose secret purpose has now been made so triumphantly clear, to you falls the honour of witnessing the fulfilment of the ancient prophecy!'

The Master still held the rack of ornamental skewers, and now he grasped one and drew it out.

'You will all be familiar with the Firedrake Codex.

But I wonder how many of you truly believe the prophecy it foretells? I was like you once. A hundred years has passed since the last of the transformed dragon-folk was put to the fire. And what were we to make of the claim that when the Silver Warrior kills the Golden Dragon we survivors of the Order would inherit the earth? Surely no more than medieval rhetoric? But behold! I bring you the champion of the Order and the last dragon on earth. I bring them before you to do battle! Will there be a thunderclap when our champion finally holds aloft the severed head of the beast? Will we find ourselves transformed to kings, presidents and potentates on the spot? I doubt it. But what I offer you tonight is a glimpse of what can be ours. Here is a fantastical conflict, acted out before your eyes, and I am the ringmaster! If this wonder has become a reality, what can we not achieve?'

Throughout this wild speech, Sam didn't once take his eyes off his enemies. Now the Master regarded Ishmael too.

'You are stronger,' he said.

'Yes, Master.' Ishmael's eyes never left Sam's; his focus didn't flicker for a moment. 'I will destroy thee!' he whispered.

'Keep faith in your Master. Do not question my actions, not for a moment.' Master Richard raised his arm and plunged the skewer into Ishmael's shoulder.

A ripple of alarmed murmurs arose from the witnesses. Sam felt the shock of the blow surge through Ishmael's body. The skewer had been tipped with a substance. The same drug Richard had used in Sam's pizza, though a much weaker quantity. Sam caught its scent and recognised it instinctively. His stomach heaved at the memory, but he didn't take his eyes off the youth with the sword. What was Master Richard doing, attacking his champion? It made no sense. But Sam wouldn't allow himself to be distracted.

Ishmael blinked.

Sam chose that moment to strike. He beat his wings, flew at the bald-headed youth, feet first, legs flailing. His claws clattered against the blade of the raised sword. He felt the cold metal against his flesh, felt it slice into his foot as he struggled to rip the weapon from his enemy's grasp. He kicked away, shot back and landed in the gravel, one foot raised, dripping blood.

Ishmael staggered backwards but stayed upright. He looked at Richard.

'Master?'

'Do not question! Let your faith answer!' The Master's voice was raised in exultation. 'The fight is everything! I cannot allow you to end it too swiftly. You will prevail, but not before the prophecy has been fulfilled.

This is a trial, a great test, not an execution! You see, witnesses! We hold sway over angels and demons, both. Look upon these wonders! They fight like animals and yet I, a man, hold the keys to victory and defeat.'

Sam swallowed. He had attacked Ishmael. He had struck when the other boy was most vulnerable. His most vicious instincts were now in control. He felt a singing in his blood. Dragon adrenalin surging through his veins. He didn't understand why Master Richard had stabbed Ishmael. He didn't care. It weakened his enemy, and so gave him an advantage. A tremor of icy fear ran through him. He was not afraid of Ishmael or Master Richard. He was afraid because he knew he was capable of killing them both. He beat his wings and leapt into the air.

Ishmael backed towards the broken door of the church. He lifted his sword. Sam felt the familiar burning in the back of his throat. He screamed, and a plume of flame shot from his mouth. Ishmael hurled himself backwards to escape the burst of fire. He fell back into the darkness of the church.

Sam followed him in, his aching jaws wide-open, spewing a shrieking tongue of flame before him. Ishmael scrambled away, swinging his sword desperately, slicing through the blasts of fire. Sam closed on him and they plunged and parried, blocked, struck, leapt and tumbled across the flagstones. The wooden pews caught light. Flames danced around the car that Crisp had driven into the church. Smoke filled the nave. Fire caught hold in the bell-tower and soon the whole building was burning.

For Sam, fire raged inside and out. It scalded his skin and his lungs and the inside of his throat and the roof of his mouth. He was consumed too, by a deeper fire, which robbed him of all restraint. He was a fire-drake, a living weapon, a thing of claws and teeth and gouts of flame. That part of him that remained a quiet boy of fourteen had been left cowering in the shadow of this wild, warring beast.

And Ishmael met him blow for blow. Seizing Sam around the waist, he bulldozed him into the stone columns of the vestibule, hammering his forehead into Sam's face again and again. Sam felt nothing. He was a living flame. He hurled Ishmael back, slashed at him with clawed fists and feet.

Flames were eating at the wooden ceiling above them. They circled, lunging at each other. Ishmael swung his sword above his head. The weapon was soot-blackened but still razor sharp. The tip of the long blade slashed against the flame-licked boards over-head. Blue sparks flew as Ishmael hacked at Sam, missed, and struck the stonework behind him.

The ceiling gave way above their heads and burning beams came crashing down around them. Ishmael staggered out through the west doorway, flames dancing about his shoulders. Back in the nave, the car exploded, adding still more violent force to the furious inferno. Sam felt the fire on his skin. It broke over him like water. He swam through the roaring flames and burst out into the cool night air.

SKEWERED

Adda-Leigh dragged herself back to the edge of the field and stopped just a few metres from the burning church. Georgette, protesting plaintively, came with her. In truth, both of them needed to see what was happening. Their lives might depend on the outcome of the fight.

The interior of the church was glowing with flickering orange firelight. The flames leapt like living things. The stained glass windows shattered and burst, one by one, and smoke poured out, darkening the night sky and making the girls choke and splutter.

Sam and Ishmael were back where the fight had begun, circling on the gravel-covered forecourt. Master Richard was waiting for them, his rack of skewers in his hands. Of the nine witnesses who had arrived in the coach only three remained. When Sam had begun spitting fire the coach driver had lost his nerve and turned on the ignition. Four of the party had leapt back on the coach before it went careering off into the night. As the fire took hold in the church, another two had broken ranks and fled across the fields. The remaining three men were gawping at the spectacle before them, slack-jawed with stupefaction. Crisp was still there, but he had fallen to the ground, his knees drawn up to his chest. He didn't appear to be moving.

'The fight must continue,' the Master said. With one swift movement he thrust a skewer into Sam's thigh. Sam's legs buckled and he sank to the ground.

In the cornfield, Adda-Leigh drew in her breath and moaned with horror.

Master Richard darted away to where Ishmael stood, his shirt smoking, a few flames still flickering around his shoulders, face and hands mottled black and red where the fire had bitten into him. The burnt youth lifted his sword. Richard drew another skewer and plunged it into Ishmael's neck.

'Too soon for the *coup de grâce*,' he said as he spun away out of reach.

'You're insane!' Sam yelled. 'Why are you doing this?'

'So that humankind may bear witness. We, the secret Order who have taken the Companions from within, we are the true champions of humanity! It is our right to rule over the world! This ceremony of death shall prove it!'

'But no one's watching! They've run away!'

Ishmael swung his sword, the blade sliced through the air. He roared out. 'I keep the faith, Master! Strike me with your darts, I shall fight on!'

'Bless you, my son!' Master Richard called back.

Adda-Leigh covered her eyes with her hands. 'Oh God,' she said.

Sam evaded the sword swipe and now advanced on Ishmael. Master Richard danced forward and hurled another skewer at him. It stuck in Sam's chest. Once again he sank to his knees.

Adda-Leigh cried out. 'They're going to kill each other!'

'Make it stop!' Georgette whispered, beside her.

JUGULAR

Georgette lifted her hand to her mouth. She felt sick. There was a smell in the air, along with the smoke. Burning skin.

There was no one else watching the battle any more. The last three witnesses had turned tail and run. Only Crisp remained, curled up in a foetal position on the gravel. Hidden in the corn, Georgette and Adda-Leigh were the only witnesses.

The bells in the blazing tower had begun a restless and confused chiming as the hot air set them swinging. Firelight illuminated the scene before her. Three figures, watching each other.

The bald-headed youth coughed painfully. He wiped blood from his mouth with the back of his hand. His head, his face, his hands, all had been charred in the fire. His clothes were still smoking. Sam's leathery hide had also suffered, burnt black in patches and textured now like coal.

But the fight wasn't over. The boy with the sword ran at Sam. Sam leapt backwards. His wings flapped uselessly at the air. He was injured, exhausted. When he landed in the gravel he fell onto his back and let out a howl of pain. Smoke and ash blew from his mouth. The sword swung through the air, bit down into the ground, scattering gravel.

Sam had rolled aside at the last moment. He was on his feet again. One of his wings hung down his back, twisted and broken, the thin flesh tattered. He tried to speak, pointing one claw-tipped finger at the white-haired man, who stood at a cautious distance, regarding the two combatants with a look of diabolical excitement. Sam's voice was no more than a choked rumble. The white-haired man laughed.

'Hear him, Ishmael? The voice of the dragon. You will silence that voice for ever, before you die. You have given your life for this battle. Your name shall live for ever. Like Beowulf, who overcame the Firedrake.'

Ishmael was struggling to pull the sword out of the ground. He tugged at the hilt but was too weak to shift it.

'Must I die, Master?' he said. His voice was that of a sorrowful child.

'You must. But not before you slay the dragon. Let me redress the balance in your favour once more, before your final push to victory!'

Ishmael's Master drew the last skewer. He held it up. The spike gleamed in the firelight.

'A little job for the last of my Five Generals!' he said.

Georgette sensed a movement at her side. Adda-Leigh had dragged herself to her feet.

'No!' Adda-Leigh's voice was wild and hoarse. Georgette too, got to her feet. Adda-Leigh took a few stumbling steps forward before collapsing on the edge of the gravel forecourt.

Sam made his last move then, in that brief moment of distraction. Lunging with desperate speed, he launched a final delirious charge that seemed to gain momentum from his imminent collapse. In one sweeping movement he seized both his tormentors by the throat, one in either hand, and pushed them back against the stones of the burning church, pinning them there.

A dog was barking, somewhere nearby. Sparks of fire were flying high into the sky. Some of the roof of the bell-tower had collapsed. There was a terrible clanking and clamouring from the bells.

Georgette saw Sam breathe in, draw up his strength. His body shook with tension. She knew what was about to happen. Sam was going to destroy his enemies. He was going to rip out their throats. She let out a moan of horror and turned her face away.

THE FIFTH GENERAL

Sam's claws closed on Master Richard's windpipe. He could snuff out this man's life in an instant. Ishmael was a tougher prospect, but the drug-tipped skewers had weakened him. Both would die; this genetically modified test-tube warrior, bred to destroy him, and this self-styled Grand Master of the New Order, survivor of the very Order that had tried to wipe out every last descendant of the people of Luhngdou. Now, at last, the dead would be avenged, and Sam would be victorious. His blood sang with merciless fury.

But inside his head there was a voice. He realised the voice had been calling, desperately, for some time, and that he'd been ignoring it. Now, in his moment of triumph, the voice made itself heard at last. Father David.

'Sam! Do not kill them! You must hold back! You must!'

Sam sensed the movement of his enemies' blood, deep in their veins and arteries. They were defenceless, both of them, his claws at their throats. But still he listened to the voice in his head.

'If you kill them, if you let the anger in you have the final word, then think what you have become! You must resist! You must be stronger than destruction. It is not your place to take life, Sam. Please! Release them! All my life I have been troubled by guilt. I have been weak and afraid, and I allowed Mrs Hare to protect me, to use violence to keep me safe. But you, Sam. You who have so much strength, so much courage, you can find another way. You must find another way!'

Sam felt a shuddering sigh pass through him and a sense of weary calm flooded his soul. He dropped his arms and stepped back from the wall. Richard and Ishmael sank to the ground, their hands massaging their throats.

Sam turned his back on them. He blinked with surprise as a dog bounded into the gravel courtyard. It was Aaron's dog, Jaws the Alsatian. This creature, which had undergone almost as many transformations as Sam himself, had followed him all the way from London. It had taken the dog many hours to get here, but here it was at last, wagging its tail in the flickering firelight.

Then Sam saw Adda-Leigh lying on the ground and he wanted to go to her. But she was yelling something, pointing. He turned and in a split-second glance he saw the Master, the open doorway of the flame-filled church at his back, the last skewer raised in his hand, about to plunge it into Sam.

Jaws sprang at the Master without a moment's hesitation. Man and dog fell into the flames. Almost simultaneously, the ring of bells collapsed and fell, crashing down through the burnt-out tower, crushing the life out of both Jaws and the Master in a single instant.

The flames in the vestibule were stifled for a moment, but then leapt up again with added vigour, roaring as if in approval of the destruction they had wrought. Sam stood rooted to the spot. He had felt the life force snuffed out of the Master and the Alsatian, like two candles stifled and left smoking. He felt hollowed out, stunned. Physical exhaustion rushed in on him and he sank to his knees.

Ishmael moved to the doorway, his bulky frame dark against the brilliance of the flames.

'Master!' he called into the inferno of the church.

Sam lifted his head. He wanted to speak, to tell this lumbering youth, this desperate warrior, that it was no good. Nobody now could enter the blazing church and come out alive, the heat was too intense.

Sam's throat was charred and dry. His tongue was swollen and he could barely swallow. He struggled to form words, but he couldn't utter a sound. Besides, surely Ishmael's senses were just as developed as Sam's? Surely he knew that his Master had perished?

'Master, come out!' Ishmael's voice was little more than a whisper, but Sam heard him, despite the roar and crackle of the fire. 'The fight is not over yet, Master. Is it a test? Must I pass through this fire?'

He turned then and looked at Sam. 'You let me live, brother,' he said. 'I shall not leave him to die.' He turned back to the church door and leapt into the flames, pushing through the blazing debris, even as he himself caught fire, and on into the body of the church itself.

Sam collapsed on the gravel. Tears ran from his eyes, and the salt water stung like acid as it dripped down the charred scales of his face. He cried for all of them.

COOL SHADOW

Adda-Leigh lay on the gravel. The heat from the fire was burning her skin. The creature that she knew to be Sam crawled across the ground and knelt beside her, panting. Its great bulk shielded her from the burning air. Smoke rose from its blackened skin.

She lifted her hand, thinking to touch its face, but the skin was blistered and raw. She couldn't bear the thought of causing Sam more pain. The creature lowered its head. Its breath came in shallow gasps.

Georgette stood a few paces away. Ishmael's sword had been left there, thrust point-first in the ground. Adda-Leigh saw Georgette place her hand on the weapon's fire-blackened hilt. The sword was nearly as long as her friend was tall.

Sam's breathing had calmed. He looked at Adda-

Leigh and she saw that his eyes were unchanged. He was the same boy he'd always been. She smiled and he bowed his great head.

The pain in her ankle was intense, and the gravel was by no means a comfortable surface to lie on, but here, in the cooling shadow of the dragon-boy's crouching bulk, Adda-Leigh felt safe for the first time in weeks. She closed her eyes and fell into a dreamless sleep.

NO SATISFACTORY EXPLANATION

Georgette knew all along that the police would not believe their story. But she knew they wouldn't have believed the truth either.

Not that either she or Adda-Leigh actually lied to the authorities. There were just certain elements of the story they left unexplained. How she'd really managed to track down the kidnapper's hiding places, for instance, and the exact cause of the fire that destroyed the abandoned church. When pressed, they just said they didn't know, or they couldn't remember. In the end, the police had to put it down to confusion brought on by the trauma of events.

Only Aaron tried to tell them everything, as far as he understood it. But he wouldn't stick to the bald facts, extraordinary as they were. He had already come to his own conclusions. But he soon found that talking to the police about dragons in the Underground wasn't the best way to be taken seriously.

A farmer had spotted the flames of the burning church and called the fire brigade. Then he'd stood and watched the conflagration from across the fields. The nearest fire station was miles away, so it had taken some while for the engines to arrive. It was too late to save what was left of the church. Georgette and Adda-Leigh had been found sitting at the edge of the cornfield, watching the building burn.

It was several days before the bodies were discovered. The church had been unused, awaiting renovation. The bell-tower, in particular, had been deemed unsafe. The congregation had moved to another church, some miles away.

There had been much lurid speculation in the press about the Adda-Leigh McDuff kidnap case, but the truth remained shrouded in mystery. There were rumours of witchcraft and black masses, and coachloads of warlocks being bussed in to attend satanic rituals. Adda-Leigh and her friend Georgette were said to have been intended as human sacrifices, but an accident with a flaming cross had resulted in the church burning down and the girls escaping death.

But neither of the girls in question ever verified these tales. They had both been found safe and, apart from Adda-Leigh's broken ankle, relatively well. In fact, Georgette had been missing for such a short time her father hadn't even become aware of her disappearance. The kidnappers, if that was who they were, both seemed to have died in the fire; there was little incentive for the police to tie up all the loose ends. An Alsatian dog, perhaps a stray that had taken refuge in the church, or maybe a guard dog belonging to the kidnappers, was the third victim of the fire, or so it was reported. There was never any mention of Crisp in any of the reports. Living or dead, no sign of him had been found near the burnt-out church.

Yet another puzzling aspect of the story lay in the fact that the twisted remains of a car had been found amidst the ruins of the church. No satisfactory explanation for that extraordinary occurrence was ever put forward.

Georgette and Adda-Leigh resolutely refused to elaborate on the vague details they'd offered the police. Adda-Leigh remained off sick for the rest of the term and planned to start at a new school in September. In August, a month after the incident, Georgette moved to York, to live with her mother.

A JOURNEY OF DISCOVERY

The journey back to Ireland was slow. Sam was healing, getting stronger day by day, but he wasn't yet fit to fly. He travelled by night, and only moved when nobody was there to see him.

Once, he glanced up at the window of a house he was passing, on the outskirts of Bristol. A small child was looking down at him, whey-faced, solemn. But the sight of a tall reptilian creature with leathery wings, standing up on two legs and limping painfully along the moonlit road didn't seem to cause the child any great consternation. Sam even chanced a wave of his clawed hand. The child's mouth twitched at the corners and formed a tentative smile. Sam walked on.

Animals no longer fled at his approach. A vixen sniffed at his hand and then trotted along at his side for several miles as he walked from hillside to hillside, avoiding the villages, heading north into Wales. A stag broke cover and acknowledged his presence with a shake of its antlered head as he passed below a wooded ridge, early one morning.

But Sam could only think of Adda-Leigh. What did she believe him to be? An animal? A monster? A freak? He had left her sleeping, had crept away when the emergency services arrived. This time, they'd not even said goodbye. He tried to stop himself thinking about her. How could there ever be anything between them?

While Sam walked, Father David talked.

'The Order was founded on an illusion, Sam. There are truths and mysteries in the universe, but their creed spoke only falsehoods and misconceptions. Their Grand Masters kept the ancient blood feud alive down the years because it helped them hold onto power. In recent times, their secret hoard of money motivated much of their behaviour. You saw the witnesses that Master Richard brought to the battle? I recognised one of them, myself, a former army major I met a long time ago. For some of those men, involvement with the Order and their infiltration of the Companions would have been undertaken purely for personal gain. I doubt many of them really believed in dragons before this evening! Some may have been less dismissive, but few of them would have believed in the prophecies of the Firedrake Codex as fervently as Master Richard did. But, as you know, he parted company with both

his sanity and with his humanity a long time ago. Do you know, some have even suggested that the Codex was a medieval forgery, a bogus biblical text put together by the founders of the Order? A tissue of lies based around a fundamental mis-understanding of beings such as yourself. Master Richard was determined to twist lies into realities.'

Sam stood on a rock-strewn hillside and looked down at the village that lay in the valley below. Father David continued to speak, warming to his theme.

'These Knights of the Pursuing Flame called themselves Christians, men of god, but their god was an invention, a fic-tion invoked to support their every desire — to justify their every wrong!' Father David broke off. *'Why have you stopped walking?'* he said.

It was Grandma Evans's village. Sam had never been there before, but he knew where he was as surely as if he'd looked it up on the map. He had been heading this way, trusting to an internal magnet that had drawn him on towards his own kin.

He knew the house, last in the street. Around the back of the building a basketball hoop had been fixed to the wall.

'That's new,' said Father David.

Sam stood still, watching the house. He came closer. His movements were infinitesimal and he remained unseen. A man in a wheelchair was playing basketball, shooting the ball into the basket with an expert aim.

'Your father looks well.'

Sam could smell no alcohol from the man throwing the basketball. He sensed an air of unaccustomed calm from his father, as well as a twinge of sadness. There were scars on his skin, from the burns he had received, but for all that he seemed a healthier man than when Sam had last seen him.

'I'm sure he misses you. You know you could stay here, if you wanted to? You are still his son . . .'

Sam said nothing. He just shook his head so slowly no passer-by would have even noticed the barest of movements in the shadows behind old Mrs Evans's house. Now was not the time.

Sam reached the coast near Harlech.

'We can't have you rattling around in my head for ever,' he said to the voice of Father David. He realised, as he spoke, that he knew the secret of Father David's imprisonment, and that he'd known it for some while, though he hadn't been conscious of it until now. It still wasn't something that was easy to believe.

'It's time to find a way of getting you released,' he said.

Father David, for once, was quiet.

Sam tested his wings for the first time since the fight at the church. As the sun rose, he swept low over the battlements of Harlech Castle. He passed over the sand-dunes heading for the sea. When he got beyond the shallows he dived into the waves and let the water take him down.

The sea salt soothed his battered hide. He swam well below the wind-whipped surface for hours at a time, rising only occasionally to take in a little more air. He headed for the south coast of Ireland.

At last, he reached the cliffs near Ballylach strand. The cottage where he and Father David had lived was only a mile or so inland. Sam dived deep.

The body was down on the seabed, floating peacefully in an upright position, legs tied fast, anchored to a lump of cement. It had been in the water for several days and only the familiar clothes enabled Father David to recognise who it was. Even then, there were still a few moments of disbelief. When the truth finally hit him, he was suddenly back in the white-walled rooms where he'd been held as a prisoner. The brass dragon had slipped out of his hand again.

STICKS AND DREAMS

Father David looked around the floor of the empty room, but the brass dragon was nowhere to be found.

He paced through the interconnected rooms. He'd grown used to the stinging in his eyes and the muffled hissing in his ears that had accompanied his continued presence at Sam's side. Now he found the absence of those symptoms disorientating.

He stubbed his toe against the wall as he passed through the door into the passageway and his boot left a scuffmark on the skirting board. He walked through to the next room. There was the scuffmark again. He hurried into the next room. Same scuffmark.

There was only one room. Father David felt panic grip him. He couldn't understand it. He couldn't think. He couldn't think about the body in the sea, down near the base of the cliffs.

He heard the seagulls crying, and the crash of the waves somewhere outside. He walked through to the next room, although he knew now that he would end up in exactly the same place.

Except this time, she was there. It was the woman he'd seen here before, always ahead of him. Now she stood waiting; a small oriental woman with a round face, like a pebble.

'Hello, David.' She smiled at him.

'It's you!' he said. 'Well, of course it is. Who else could you be?' He laughed, then stammered, and felt his cheeks burning with embarrassment. How foolish he sounded. Who was she?

'I think you know who I am,' she said.

He stared at her. 'What is this place?'

She ignored the question. 'I'd like to thank you for helping Sam. You were with him when he needed you most.'

'It was nothing, I mean, I was nothing. Just a voice.' He trailed off.

'What are we ever but "just a voice"?' she said. 'A mere consciousness, a collection of imprecise memories, a cluster of pulsing neurons. Such things are transferable, for a while at least. He wasn't aware of it, but Sam didn't want to lose you, didn't want to be left alone. He is only a boy, after all. So, at the moment of your death, he took you, transferred your consciousness into his, like downloading a file off the Internet. And he kept you with him. Kept you with him, until now . . .'

'My death? So, Master Richard . . .?'

'Yes.' Her expression was mournful. 'I'm sorry.'

'But this place, these rooms. You. It all seems so real!'

'Seeming real is not enough,' she said. 'You know that, David. A straight stick, when placed in a glass of water, may appear to be bent. And to the dreamer, a dream can have the absolute semblance of reality.'

Father David looked at her. 'Who are you?' he said.

She didn't answer him. 'Sticks can be taken out of water,' she said. 'Dreams can come to an end.'

She stood aside then, and he saw there was a door in the wall behind her, a door that had not been there before. The handle had a well-worn look to it, smooth and shiny brass, polished by the grip of many hands.

'Am I to go through?' he asked the woman.

She nodded.

Father David sighed. He was glad, he realised. Since Mrs Hare died, he had been floundering, a rudderless ship. Now, at last, he knew what he was supposed to do.

'Tell me,' he said, moving towards the door, 'will Sam . . . ?' He broke off, somehow unable to complete the question.

'When he needs me, I shall be here,' she said.

Father David understood at last. 'You are Suzi Lim-Evans! You are Sam's mother,' he said.

She nodded, solemn now. It was Father David who smiled.

'I'm very pleased to have met you,' he said. He grasped the door handle and turned it. There was a soft click, and the door swung open.

Sam felt the change immediately. Father David was a presence no more. The little priest did not vanish in a puff of air. Rather it was the way Sam thought about him that subtly altered. He cooled and solidified in Sam's mind, became a story, with a beginning, a middle and an end, complete in itself, finished. If he ever heard Father David's voice again, Sam knew it would be from within the confines of his memory. The transformation was over in the time it took to open and close a door.

Sam freed the priest's body and let the tide carry it towards the strand. Without breaking surface, he turned from the shore and swam away through the turgid waters of the channel. He headed north.

GOODBYES

It was Aaron who came to see Georgette off at the station. Even though he'd said he 'wasn't good with goodbyes'. Her dad was working and Adda-Leigh was at home with her parents. They still couldn't bear to let her out of their sight. And besides, she was on crutches, her ankle encased in plaster. But she'd promised to come up to York to visit in October.

'We got her back then, didn't we?' Aaron said. He leant against the side of the carriage. Georgette struggled to lift her heavy suitcase. Panting with exertion, she slid it in through the carriage door.

'We got old Adda-Leigh back again, you and me,' Aaron continued. 'Not a bad team, eh?'

Georgette climbed up after her suitcase and turned in the doorway, looking at Aaron. He squinted up at her. Reaching into his trouser pocket, he pulled out a battered-looking Mars Bar.

'Here,' he said. 'For the journey.' He tossed her the bar, and Georgette caught it automatically. It was soft, and unpleasantly warm.

'I'm still gutted about old Jaws though.' Aaron puckered his brows. 'I know he was a right wimp and all that, but I miss him now he's gone.'

'He was fearless,' Georgette said, seriously. 'He was a hero.'

'Yeah,' said Aaron. 'But when it comes down to it, who wants to be a dead hero?'

Doors began to slam all along the length of the train.

'Goodbye,' Georgette said. She tried to sound non-chalant, but ended up sounding rather colder than she'd meant. Aaron didn't seem bothered. Standing on the platform, he performed an extravagant and sweep-ing bow.

'Farewell!' he said, in a booming voice, jiggling his eyebrows up and down for comic effect. Georgette allowed him a smile. She thought she owed him a smile at least.

As the train pulled out of the station and Georgette settled into her seat, it occurred to her that, contrary to what he'd said, Aaron didn't seem to be all that bad at goodbyes.

KNIGHTS AND DRAGONS

Four Weeks Later

Adda-Leigh stood on the paving stones below York Minster and looked up. Georgette had met her at the station and they'd walked up through the town centre, getting used to each other's company again. It was over a month since they'd last met.

'I like your top,' Adda-Leigh said. She pinched the fabric of her friend's sleeve. Georgette frowned and tugged at the hem, pulling it downwards.

'Mum bought it for me. It's too short.'

'It's meant to be like that, girl!' Adda-Leigh smiled. 'Your mum's got better fashion sense than you have.'

'Don't I know it!' Georgette rolled her eyes. 'She's always dragging me round the shops.'

'Sounds all right to me,' Adda-Leigh said.

Georgette looked at her. 'I can see I might regret inviting you up here. Especially if you decide to team up with my mum!'

Adda-Leigh grinned, then looked concerned. 'It's okay though, isn't it? I mean, you living up here with your mum?'

Georgette shrugged. 'I'm getting used to it.'

'And your mum's boyfriend, and his kids, what are they like?'

'Okay, I suppose.'

'They're not going to mind, are they? I mean what I told you, about me having to sleep with the light on and all that?' Adda-Leigh looked anxiously at Georgette.

'They're fine with it, honestly.'

'And I have to have the bedroom door open at night, and a light on in the hall. I'm sorry.' Adda-Leigh chewed her lip. 'You must think I've totally lost it.'

'Come on, Addie,' Georgette said. 'It's me. I know what you've been through. Everyone's okay. They're looking forward to meeting you. They're all really nice and it's going to be fine. The twins have crammed into the boxroom so you can have the biggest bedroom to yourself. Should help with the claustrophobia.'

Adda-Leigh gave a rueful laugh. 'Thanks,' she said. 'I get in a bit of a panic sometimes, that's all.' She changed the subject. 'What's the town like?'

'The river's okay. And this place is pretty amazing.' Georgette tipped her head to indicate the vast, cream-coloured edifice of the Minster, towering above them.

Adda-Leigh gazed up at the ornate parapets and pinnacles, the flying buttresses and jutting gargoyles.

'I don't know,' she said. 'I've kind of gone off church architecture.' The girls grinned at each other, then a more solemn look passed between them.

'Come on.' It was Georgette who broke the silence. 'It's not far to my house.'

But Adda-Leigh lingered a while in the shadow of the Minster. She looked up at the carvings, high on the walls. Saintly looking knights and leering dragons, the old prejudice.

Something caught her eye. A movement? She wasn't sure. She squinted up at the pale cream stones. What had made her look up? She felt it still, a pull, like something brushing against her, lighter than a touch, fainter than a breath of air.

She stood under the Minster walls for a long while. Georgette waited patiently. Adda-Leigh kept her head tipped, looking up until the back of her neck hurt, but she could see nothing there.

THE THREAD

At the highest point on the Minster tower Sam stood, frozen into stillness. He looked at the people below. They were as small as ants and he was invisible to them all. He knew for certain now that he was no longer one of them.

They seemed so small from this height, but each of them was a living being, with all the needs and ambitions, hopes and fears, friends, relations and acquaintances that life brought them. Each of them moved through time, heading towards their own particular destiny, trailing all their thoughts and memories, like banners behind them. Until, like Father David, like Ishmael and Master Richard, like a fearless dog called Jaws, they arrived at their ending.

Sam looked at the people in the town below and

knew that one of them was Adda-Leigh. She seemed to be looking up at him, though he was sure he couldn't be seen.

He didn't know what he was going to do, not today, not tomorrow, not now, not any time. Neither could he imagine where he was going to go. He was as rootless as the wind. And yet one thing he did know was that there was now an unbreakable thread, invisible and infinite in its reach, which connected him to Adda-Leigh. He felt the tug of it now, but knew he couldn't answer its call. She was human, whereas he was . . .

Moving so slowly no eye could detect him, Sam leant forward and laid his forehead gently against the cold stone of the great tower.